Mack Bolan heard the groans

Rage made him close in on the moaning, blazing a trail of death as he went. Bodies littered the floor.

He hurdled the fallen flesh, then sent two hundred pounds of raging kick into the door. His Thompson up and ready, he stormed through in a burst of splinters...

...and stopped dead in his tracks.

Before him was a blood-drenched torture chamber of stench and carnage. Bolan had entered a living hell.

Other
MACK BOLAN
titles in the Gold Eagle
Executioner series

#39 The New War
#40 Double Crossfire
#41 The Violent Streets
#42 The Iranian Hit
#43 Return to Vietnam
#44 Terrorist Summit
#45 Paramilitary Plot
#46 Bloodsport
#47 Renegade Agent

Mack Bolan's
ABLE TEAM

#1 Tower of Terror
#2 The Hostaged Island
#3 Texas Showdown

Mack Bolan's
PHOENIX FORCE

#1 Argentine Deadline
#2 Guerilla Games
#3 Atlantic Scramble

MACK

THE EXECUTIONER 48

BOLAN

The Libya Connection

A GOLD EAGLE BOOK FROM

WORLDWIDE

TORONTO · NEW YORK · LONDON

First edition December 1982

ISBN 0-373-61048-3

Special thanks and acknowledgment to
Stephen Mertz for his contribution to this work.

Printed in Canada

The essential American is a man who keeps
his moral integrity hard and intact,
an isolate, almost selfless, stoic enduring man
who lives by death.
                                        —*D. H. Lawrence*

For mere vengeance I would do nothing.
This nation is too great to look for mere revenge.
But for the security of the future I would do everything.
                                        —*James Garfield*

I live on the razor's edge that separates the living
from the dead. Vengeance is not my sword. I fight
only for the future of us all, and it is
an endless fight.
                                        —*Mack Bolan, The Executioner*
                                        (from his journal)

Dedicated to the victims of the Beirut massacre.

1

It was almost dawn.

The 125-foot yacht, ghostly silent, rode the calm surface of Exuma Cay, 230 nautical miles southeast of Miami. The smoothness of the water was like dark glass.

It did not look to be a scene just minutes short of shattering into hellfire and destruction.

But it was.

The big man broke the water's surface fifteen feet below the "pleasure craft's" stern.

He moved soundlessly from stern to bow, then wrapped hands and ankles around the heavy chain of the boat's anchor line. The dripping of the water was the first sound he had made.

Bolan moved as one with the darkness. He hoisted himself upward, rapidly.

The nightscorcher was outfitted for a hard, fast hit. At his right hip rode the formidable .44 Auto-Mag, "Big Thunder." Beneath his left arm was the 9mm Beretta Brigadier equipped with a silencer of Bolan's own design. Both weapons were protected by snap-sealed waterproof holsters. Hardpunch munitions rode dry in the waterproof pouch at his left hip. The slit pockets of his blacksuit carried garrotes and small knives. The suit, designed to Bolan's specifications, was skintight, nothing to get snagged or impede movement.

He dropped, catlike, onto the boat's deck.

The predawn stillness appeared undisturbed.

Bolan fisted the Beretta Belle. He eased into a crouch, scanning the deck to encompass all that might lurk there.

Thirty feet separated him from a companionway that led below deck. Just beyond the open hatch was the gray slab of a helicopter landing pad, twenty feet by fifteen feet. Beyond that, the deck stretched to the main cabin and the bridge. A radar dish, turning endlessly, was dimly visible there.

Bolan could make out the forms of two men standing watch behind the windows of the wheelhouse. He saw the pinpoint glow of a cigarette.

He sprinted low and fast toward the hatchway. His black shoes were designed to make no sound, wet or dry. He reached the hatchway and disappeared into it.

Aboard this yacht there was a Puerto Rican agent, and she was known to Mack Bolan.

Known and respected.

And loved.

Bolan moved with the swift advantage of prior intel to a below-deck companionway that led to the fuel tanks. He paused briefly beside the tanks and unsnapped the waterproof pouch at his left hip, withdrawing a plastic-wrapped clump of plastique explosive that he wedged in between the tanks and the hull. He inserted a timer fuse, set the detonation cap for five minutes, then continued on into the companionway, toward the sound of murmuring voices.

Masculine, relaxed sounds.

The companionway was carpeted a plush red, further muffling his approach.

The human sounds led him two doors down, to his left. He reached the closed door.

A kick that sent the wood panel splintering inward off its hinges powerhoused him through.

The Executioner went in low, the Beretta up and spitting.

Mack Bolan was here to deliver the final tab from Mother Universe for a lifetime of violent and merciless exploitation.

The yacht *Traveler* was owned by financier Leonard J. Jericho—fugitive financier, financier Puerto Rico-style.

Jericho was Bolan's target.

The Executioner had long been aware of Lenny Jericho and the man's shadowy dealings in high places. The name had come up more than once during Bolan's previous war.

But Jericho was always an illusive presence: a vicious, hungry cannibal, the same age as Bolan, who personally directed a widespread web of activities (read: crimes) from any number of secret bases around the world that neither the authorities nor the majority of Jericho's own associates could ever identify.

For Bolan it was simple cat and mouse. Easy to identify, easy to hit, easy to git. Easy to mark up as one more scene for Stony Man to cleanse while the authorities blinded themselves with dollar signs and international law.

Except that Bolan would never have allied himself with the get-Jericho forces if his own ally was not personally imperiled. That made it a whole different game.

Jericho was under federal indictment charging him with looting an estimated three hundred million dollars from Paris-based Investors International Services Limited. The globe-trotting financier was also accused by Senate investigators of masterminding a thirty-million-dollar bribe network that had reached into the White House itself during two recent administrations.

The CIA also suspected him of Central American gunrunning.

Jericho had the money and the brains to stay out of the picture, yet he controlled the picture itself, bartering souls with an impunity bought by bribery, fear, murder.

Thanks to the Puerto Rican authorities, the Justice Department had finally gotten a handle on Jericho. The man was tolerated but not loved in his place of exile. The guy's connections to international organized crime were particularly visible in both Puerto Rico and the Bahamas, and the rumors were that Jericho had been busy establishing a new heroin pipeline for the tattered remains of some of the U.S. Mafia families.

The Puerto Ricans had eventually planted an undercover agent in the middle echelon of the Jericho Bahamas organization, and the agent had picked up tremors of something of even greater import.

The agent's name was Evita Aguilar.

Eve was Bolan's friend and she had been his lover.

She possessed the unmistakable capacity for living large.

Bolan had first met the female firestorm during his war against the Mafia, when the Executioner hunted down the Mob's Caribbean Carousel to the Glass Bay stronghold of Vince Triesta.

During the flight south for this rescue today, names and scenes of violence from long-ago action had flashed in Bolan's memory: Quick Tony Lavagni, Triesta, Riappi, the brutal firefights that had seen their end....

And Eve Aguilar, the beautiful, gutsy, tender woman who had played a vital role in aiding Bolan destroy the Caribbean plans going down at the time.

That very special lady held permanent claim to a large part of this warrior's large heart.

Bolan was aboard the now-doomed floating charnel house off Exuma Cay to rescue his kind of woman. And to ensure no replay by the hoods who held her.

This was not a rescue mission like with Toby Ranger, who had become involved once the mission was under way.

This was a mission occasioned by a friend from the very outset.

This was a personal mission with a vengeance.

Bolan was supposed to be on R & R to speed recovery from some badly ripped-open flesh inflicted by a misinformed rookie in London, England. Thanks to the doctors in London and back home in Virginia, Mack Bolan a.k.a. Colonel John Phoenix of the new Terrorist Wars was healing well—too well to stay at home. Rest and goddamned recreation was out of the question, he had told Hal Brognola. Forget it. Hear the real world, Hal.

Bolan did not listen to his liaison officer's woeful predictions about the real world of good health. Instead he listened to bitter news. It was news played to him hourly by the monitoring computers of his organization. It was the data that had brought him here to this unhealthy boat. Sufficient data to launch a search and rescue: self-evident, self-justifying. Like all bad news about good people, it was a call to action.

Eve's agency had not heard from her in seven days. Too long. Eve had been sucked into the Jericho operation, her cover probably blown.

Bolan was here to do whatever damage he could to the unfolding Jericho scam...which, under the circumstances, would be considerable.

They had Eve.

Bolan was *not* here to give quarter.

2

Three men were sitting around a table playing cards. The air had become stale and hazy with cigarette and cigar smoke. A naked low-watt bulb cast the walls and corners of the room in dark shadow.

The men were all armed.

They were all fast.

But they were not fast enough.

Bolan plugged an ugly, scarred Puerto Rican with an even uglier hole through the head. The shot sent the guy spiraling backward from his chair into the corner, a hand still wrapped tight around the butt of a shoulder-rigged .357.

The second guy was big, and fast enough that he managed to fill his fist with a P-35 Browning hipower and track it around on Bolan, before death from the Beretta stopped him cold. He was kicked back in a deadfall slide to join the first corpse.

In microseconds Bolan sidestepped deeper into the crew's quarters, deep in the belly of Lenny Jericho's yacht. The third guy, an Arab, had lunged for a sawed-off Remington 870 pump shotgun that was positioned on the floor near his chair.

He never made it.

The Beretta sneezed a third time.

A third man died.

Not one of them knew what in hell had come exploding through that door.

Bolan straightened. He saw a wall of personal lockers, another with a row of bunks.

And he saw one lower bunk, separate from the others, built into the far bulkhead.

Gliding over the three dead men, he moved over to it and made a cursory inspection of the bunk.

It was indeed different from the others. Heavy chain shackles that ended in braces were built in to imprison the occupant by wrists and ankles. Rough blankets were in twisted disarray, indicating a recent struggle.

Tiny red droplets on the mattress screamed in Bolan's eye. He reached down and touched the stains with a fingertip.

Blood. Still sticky.

He hustled back into the corridor, to his left now, along the narrow walkway toward midship.

He slowed his pace when he reached the hatchway that led up to the deck. Then in silent, ghostlike manner he mounted the hatchway steps. He was halfway to the companionway when the opening was fully filled with the bulky form of a crewman toting an ugly FN Model 49.

Bolan pulled off two rounds, head shots. The man was propelled backward as if pulled by invisible forces. Bolan holstered the Beretta and unlimbered the mighty AutoMag as he continued on up the steps.

He erupted onto the deck, then wove a brisk zig-zag pattern across the forty feet that separated him from cover at the base of the wheelhouse superstructure.

The second guard, partner of the late creep with the FN, had not left his post behind the windows of the wheelhouse. The guard spotted the black-clad figure in the dawn's early light before Bolan had gone five paces.

The guard leaned through an open window and opened fire. A NATO round splintered the planking of the deck where Bolan had been a split-second earlier.

Bolan halted his course, in the same movement bringing up Big Thunder on the guard's silhouette on the bridge, and squeezed off a round from a two-handed target-range stance. The blazing issue of the mini-howitzer ruptured the guard's skull into a misty pink shower. The guy toppled down and out of sight.

Silence reclaimed the dawn.

Bolan gained the base of the superstructure. He knew that half his allotted time had run out since planting the five-minute fuse on the plastique.

Bolan heard a dull bump on the port side.

He responded with economy of movement. He circled the wheelhouse and cabin and came around a corner on the far side of the superstructure, just as Leonard Jericho was reaching over to activate the lowering mechanism for the lifeboat in which he was standing.

The bump was the hull of the lifeboat clunking against the yacht as Jericho clambered aboard.

Lenny was not alone.

His co-passenger was a heavyset guy, in his fifties, dressed in a five-hundred-dollar suit that was as out of place as hailstones in these surroundings.

Bolan quit the safety of cover with no attempt at secrecy. Still drenched, but silent as a wraith, he approached the lifeboat.

The two men sensed their executioner's presence. They glanced in unison toward him and their eyes widened.

The guy in the sharkskin suit reacted first.

He was Manny Mandone. Bolan recognized him from his Dixie mop-up.

Right now the Mafia shark was trying to negotiate too many things at once: turning around in the small boat, trying to maintain his equilibrium, reaching for his hardware.

The AutoMag belched flame from Bolan's fist, the heavy round tearing flesh and bone. Manny Mandone toppled over the side of the lifeboat with an astonished look on his face and a baseball-sized cavity where his heart had been.

Leonard Jericho did not move except to glance over the side, ever so briefly, after Mandone. Then he looked back at Mack Bolan.

Bolan recognized him from the intel dossier. Ten

years ago, Jericho had been movie-star handsome. But now that he was assessed to be the third or fourth richest man in the world, layers of dissipated flab had been added to the financier's features.

A heartbeat pause.

"Get out of the boat," said Bolan. His voice had the same command of Jericho's attention as the extended barrel of the AutoMag. The seconds were running out on the plastique.

Jericho obeyed. He climbed from the lifeboat. A patina of sweat glistened below his hairline despite the coolness of the early hour.

"I don't know who sent you," Jericho said. "But I can double whatever you're getting."

"I want Evita Aguilar," growled Bolan.

Jericho blinked. "Evita? She's not here."

"Where is she?"

"Who sent you? I'll triple whatever you've been paid. If you're working for the Libyans—"

A noise came from the northeast.

Grimaldi, coming in for the pickup. Right on schedule.

Which meant there were seventy-five seconds remaining before the plastique blew.

Leonard Jericho did not appreciate that the approaching helicopter was not his. Victory flashed in his eyes.

Bolan triggered the AutoMag, blowing away Jericho's left ankle, effectively amputating his foot.

They had Eve. No quarter would be given.

Bolan stepped forward and knelt atop the stunned, silently shrieking man, pinning Jericho's neck to the deck with his leg. He grabbed a handful of Jericho's hair and banged the back of the guy's head down hard to get some more of his attention.

"I want Evita. Tell me where she is."

The financier gasped for air. The pain of his shredded ankle was numbed by breathtaking shock. Blood pulsed from the wound, swilling around bone shards to form a widening puddle on the deck.

"Evita was taken from here. . . an hour ago. . . ."

"Where to?"

"I swear to God I don't know! Santos. . . took her. Libya? Business finished here. . . Thatcher was aboard last night. . . paid and gone. . . ."

Time was running out. But this man was talking. *Too* much.

"You're not Jericho."

"Let me live, please, I beg you!"

"I'm here to collect dues from Jericho."

"I'm not Jericho, you're right. . . you said it yourself."

Surprise.

Jack Grimaldi was hovering at two o'clock off the *Traveler*'s port bow. The bubble-front of the Hughes 500-D chopper reflected the rays of a new Bahamas day. A secured rope ladder dropped from the copter's side door.

Fourteen seconds to detonation.

Bolan could not allow the talkative Jericho impostor to die here. He was invaluable now for the information he could give about the boss cannibal. And about Eve, which is where Bolan came in.

The guy was losing plenty of blood. A tourniquet in the chopper, a quick airlift to medical help, and he would be fine for some hard questions.

Suddenly the guy went for broke and rolled his dice one last time. A Colt .38 snubnose was in his fist, yanked from concealment and zeroing in on Bolan.

Eleven seconds.

The Executioner darted to the right. The AutoMag and the guy's .38 fired as one. The wounded man's slug went wild. Bolan's did not.

Ten seconds.

Whoever the impostor really was, his meat was nailed to the boat's deck by a .44 headbuster that had ended his life forever.

His stupidly unthought-out course of action had confirmed for sure that he was not Lenny Jericho.

Bolan leathered Big Thunder and sidestepped the latest dead man. Timing was everything now.

He climbed the railing of the *Traveler*'s side and dived. It was a dive that expertly knifed the glassy waters of Exuma Cay to propel him down deep.

The underwater concussion from the exploding yacht was painful, like being hit by a steel door. But it lacked the shrapnel of hot yacht pieces and hurtling ice picks of fire that would have deafened and

torn him if his dive had been shallow and he had sur-
faced one second prematurely.

He broke surface as debris from the disintegrated
Traveler sizzled in the water about him.

A blown-out hulk was all that remained of Lenny
Jericho's yacht and those dead men aboard it. The
hulk began to sink as Bolan watched.

Grimaldi held the Hughes in a low hover, directly
over Bolan's head, with the rope ladder dangling
within easy reach. Bolan gripped the ladder and
began pulling himself upward from a sea made suddenly choppy by the rotors. Grimaldi eased them
away from there with a gentle increase of power.

The waters of Exuma Cay pulled away below him.
The sea was a dark turquoise blue, tabletop smooth
again in the rising sun as if nothing had happened.

Bolan preferred it that way.

He tugged himself up to the last rung of the rope
ladder and hoisted himself into the bubble-front
chopper.

"More pestilence of fire, Colonel Phoenix!"
beamed Stony Man's premier flyer. "You nearly
blasted me away from you forever."

"Should have ducked like I did," smiled Bolan.
"You knew I was going to thunder it."

"That I did," said Grimaldi, subtly maneuvering
the controls as if the whirlybird was a part of him. He
glanced at Bolan through silvered glasses.

"You got wet. Anything else?"

"Yes and no," muttered Bolan. "The yes turned

out to be a no, so to hell with him." He pushed his damp hair back from his brow, unzipped the top of his blacksuit. "To hell with anyone who comes between me and Eve. To hell with them."

"Got you," nodded Grimaldi, well aware of the grim message in Mack's soft-spoken words. "Just point me where you want me to go."

3

It was late afternoon.

Heavy draperies shuttered out the cool winter sunshine from the Stony Man War Room. The only illumination was reflected off a screen that dominated one wall.

Bolan had returned to Stony Man from the Bahamas a short twenty-five minutes earlier. The lightweight Hughes, equipped with auxiliary fuel tanks for distance, had sped them over reefs of sand and coral, then over the lush tropical forests of scattered islands, at speeds of over 150 knots to a government airfield outside Miami, Florida.

At this moment, Jack Grimaldi was ensuring that the F-14 Tomcat jet, which had flown them to Washington from Miami, was readied for further short notice.

Three people, besides Bolan, were present at the briefing.

Aaron Kurtzman. Hal Brognola. April Rose.

The screen was filled with the image of a male face. The visage was highlighted by hard eyes and a scar down the left cheek.

Kurtzman's well-modulated voice supplied the data.

"Raoul Santos. Lenny Jericho's people found him doing life for a double knife murder in Kingston involving the *rasta* drug trade. A contract job. The wife and child of a government investigator were tortured before he cut their throats. That was the only time he was ever caught. There's plenty more, if you want to hear it. They call him 'The Butcher.'"

"How long has he been with Jericho?" Bolan cut in.

"Jericho paid the guy's way out of the slammer in 1980," supplied Hal. "Jericho takes great care to keep the connection secret. The media image Jericho has created for himself is some sort of a modern Robin Hood. He's almost a folk hero—the smart con artist who got away."

April could not take her eyes away from the face of Santos on the screen.

"A mother and child.... What does he do for Jericho?"

"Whatever dirty work needs doing," said Hal, "and there's plenty of that in Jericho's world."

"And Santos has Eve," grunted Bolan. "What about the Thatcher character?"

Kurtzman punched up another head shot, this time front and profile.

It was a craggy face dominated by steely eyes that were impossible to read. The jawline was that of a determined military man in middle age.

"General Arnold L. Thatcher," said Kurtzman. "I put through a tracer when the computer kicked his name out, and the Pentagon's Internal Affairs Division was very interested in what we wanted to know and why. They're in it with us now.

"The general is chief of security at a classified base in the Rockies, north of Denver. The installation is a storage depot—part of the army's NCB program."

Bolan knew those initials. Nuclear, Chemical and Biological.

He scrutinized the frontal portrait on the screen. He saw a brokenness and a cynicism in the face that stared blankly back.

"Thatcher is two days into a five-day leave and no one's been able to run him down yet," reported Brognola. "But considering his sensitive position in the NCB program, the Pentagon and the CIA are of course giving this top priority and we should have our hands on this bad general soon enough.

"Internal Affairs launched a backtrack investigation and they came up with a bombshell this afternoon that confirms he's the Thatcher we're looking for.

"The general took a medical leave late last year. His hospital records showed treatment for stomach problems that were supposedly cleared up. But the Pentagon investigators found more—they asked the right questions of the right people in the right way.

"General Thatcher has seven months to live. He's dying of cancer. He's ripe for a sellout. Maybe he's trying to establish financial security for his family after he's gone.''

General Thatcher's likeness disappeared from the briefing-room screen. Comfortable indirect lighting filled the room.

Bolan spoke first.

"Jericho bought something from Thatcher, or paid Thatcher to do something.''

"The connection is Libya,'' said Kurtzman. "Those are the Jericho impostor's words. And Hal's got major information coming up.''

Bolan lit a cigarette.

"I think Eve Aguilar pieced the whole thing together,'' he said. "Manny Mandone was aboard the yacht. There was a lot of strange stuff going on. And she knows all about it.''

Kurtzman turned from processing continuing data.

"I'm glad to hear that the woman is thought to be alive. But why is she alive? She should be dead. I don't mean to be brutal, but we must consider this.''

Bolan felt the bitter taste in his mouth that he had experienced throughout the flight north from Exuma Cay.

"They've taken her to Libya,'' he said. "That's where Jericho is and that's where Santos is.''

"Then...it dead-ends there, doesn't it?'' asked April, sadly.

"Not at all, unfortunately,'' growled Hal. "In a strange way it ties in with the renegade operation you just busted up, Striker. The Company feels that too many ex-CIA personnel have turned up recently working for Khaddafi, among others who have no love for us. One of the men the Company has been watching is a young retiree, name of Michael Rideout. Rideout served two military tours overseas, the second time with Special Forces. Then came his years with the CIA, out of their Marseilles office. He's been 'retired' since the Company turned him loose during a Senate investigation. The man is bored, broke and bitter."

Brognola paused to light the half-done stogie that was wedged between his chubby fingers, thought better of it.

"Rideout is our key to the Jericho operation. Listen to this. Rideout was approached four days ago by people representing Leonard Jericho. He was paid ten thousand dollars and told to stay on call to leave the country. Rideout—and our people who had him wired—received that call last night, Striker, while you and Jack were on your way to the Bahamas to do your own thing with the yacht. He caught the next commercial flight to Libya.

"Like the Bear said, all of the agencies are cooperating on this because of the NCB tie-in. The CIA people were notified at the other end and they intercepted Rideout when he landed in Benghazi this morning. They're holding him now.

"We could do what Able Team did so successfully in their Texas showdown recently—ride in on a nowhere man.

"What I'm saying is, you could take Michael Rideout's place."

Bolan stood. He turned to Kurtzman.

"Bear, I want a full printout on Thatcher, Jericho and the current situation in Libya. I need to study it on the flight over."

"You've got it," said Kurtzman.

Bolan looked back at Hal.

Hal looked from Bolan to April Rose and decided to relight his cigar.

The lovely "boss lady" of Stony Man Farm stood from the couch and walked to Bolan, then wordlessly bowed her face and touched her forehead to his mouth. The natural scent of her was strong in his nostrils, yet subtle and provocative.

His arms encircled her shapely waist and held her to him.

"What is it, lady?" he asked comfortingly. "We should be used to saying goodbye by now. It goes with the job, you know that."

"I do know it," she whispered. "But I also know that this mission is different for you. You've told me how much you and Eve mean to each other."

"What Eve and I had together was before you came along, I've told you that too," he said gently.

"You big, beautiful man," she said. "I'm not jealous, Mack. I'm only trying to tell you that I'm worried about you for the same reason that Hal is. And I think Eve must be a very special human being for you to care about her the way you do."

"She is special, April. So are you, for understanding."

"Just one promise," said April Rose. "Bring the both of you back safely, okay?"

Bolan kissed her forehead.

It was time to commence preparations for the mission to Libya.

Final preparations, as they always were for The Executioner.

April held Bolan's hand for a heartbeat more, then released it.

"On your way if you must, Colonel Phoenix," she said. "And I know you must, Mack."

And she released him.

4

Bolan's fellow passengers from Tunis had included well-dressed European businessmen, casually attired British and American oil-field workers, at least two dozen other professional-looking Westerners, many of whom would have similarly attired welcoming parties awaiting them at Benghazi.

No one met "Michael Rideout" at the Benghazi airport.

Bolan was wearing worn denim and work shirt, the uniform of the American oil-field worker abroad. He had one carry-on piece of luggage.

He emerged from the air terminal into the arid, 120-plus-degree midday heat. Libya was booming.

A row of shiny new taxis were parked in the terminal loading zone. Bolan hired one for the ride into the city. He observed with curiosity this Mediterranean powder-keg country.

Upon touchdown in the army transport plane at Tunis, Bolan had regretfully entrusted his Beretta and AutoMag to Jack Grimaldi for temporary safekeeping. Mike Rideout would not be carrying heat on a commercial flight.

Bolan knew that he would be provided with firearms as soon as he made contact, as Rideout, with Jericho's people here in Libya. Until then he was armed with a knife, purchased from a street merchant outside the airport, worn concealed at the small of his back.

Most of the houses along the dusty, palm-lined "highway" into Benghazi were timeless mud-brick affairs. Street signs and all advertisements were in Arabic, but indications of Western-style prosperity were everywhere.

In the city proper, the streets became clogged with an uncomfortable number of Japanese, American and European cars.

Traditional Arabic architecture gave way to towering glass-walled office buildings

Everywhere Bolan looked, there was movement, energy and commerce. And oppressive heat.

The country's oil fields made Libya the world's ninth largest producer. Of all the Arab nations, Libya had used its oil as a political weapon more than any other.

It was incredibly inflated profits that fueled the heavy activity in trade and housing and industrialization that Bolan saw all around him.

Government-owned and -subsidized supermarkets and stores were rapidly replacing the ancient tangled bazaars.

Libya's population, predominantly Arab Muslims, never thought that they would ever have it this good.

Of course, there was a price.

And his name was Khaddafi.

The Company's Benghazi cover operation was a
small accounting firm that serviced many of the
second-string U.S. business concerns in Libya.

The offices of Mid-Am Incorporated were in the
old section of the city, on a hillside of narrow, winding lanes that only donkeys and pedestrians could
negotiate, where the poor lived crowded together
amid occasional small business fronts that shared the
crumbling, antiquated stone architecture.

Mid-Am's quarters were behind such a storefront.
The glass had been painted black. Only the silver let-
tering on the painted glass door indicated that this
storefront was occupied at all.

The flow of the street scene before the storefront
seemed unconcerned and unaware of Mid-Am Inc.
The storefront was around the corner from the neigh-
borhood *Bah el atouk*, the Street of Merchants. The
sounds clearly carried of grocers in their open-air
stalls, all enthusiastically and simultaneously pro-
claiming the virtues of green figs, pomegranates,
lemons, oranges, almonds. All around, under blue
skies but in the shade from the throbbing sun, buzzed
the added hubbub of foot traffic in and out of scores
of craft shops specializing in jewelry and leatherwork
and shoemaking. Berber music from flutes and goat-
skin drums filled the air.

Even along this narrow side street fronting the

offices of Mid-Am, which was little more than a cob-
bled footpath, the scene bustled with local women
clad in traditional veils, on their way to or from
the market, and the Arab men—Berbers, Kabyles,
Mzabites and Bedouins—wearing the *burnous*, a
hooded mantle, all pushing, shoving, chattering their
way about their business.

Within the desultory building, the offices of Mid
Am were a modern complex of "work areas" that
housed just one cell in a network of covert CIA
operations in Libya.

The head man of the Benghazi facility was an
amiable Bostonian named Lansdale. At least, that
was what he said his name was. Bolan met the guy
after passing through two separate security check-
points that blocked his path in the facility.

Grim-faced men and some women hurried busily
about their errands, answering phones, checking files.

Lansdale showed "John Phoenix" to the sound-
proofed cell in one of the basement work areas where
the real Michael Rideout was being detained.

Bolan gazed in upon the Spartanly furnished, not
uncomfortable, room and saw the renegade American stretched out in a sedated sleep.

Ten minutes after his arrival at the Company offices, Mack Bolan was alone with Lansdale in the
head agent's office in the back of the building.

"The first piece of classified news I have for you is
that Pentagon investigators tracked down General
Thatcher stateside," said Lansdale. "Unfortunately,

the general is not doing any talking. The coded communiqué we received says he got his hands on a gun and blew his brains out. Before any questioning got under way."

Bolan fired a cigarette. He had hoped that Thatcher would have the best clue to the whereabouts of Eve Aguilar. But that hope was now dead, like the general himself.

"Tell me about Rideout," said Bolan. "What did you learn from him?"

"Ah, truth serum, it's wonderful stuff," said Lansdale. "Jericho owns a villa forty miles southeast of here in Bishabia. Rideout says that's where he was headed. He was supposed to contact the villa when he landed in Benghazi."

"That was this morning?"

"Yes. Rideout told us that a mercenary named Kennedy is honchoing the operation at the villa. They'll want to know why you're late. But air travel is notorious in these parts, and you can build a story around that."

"Does Rideout have any idea what Jericho's operation is all about?"

"Negative. He was told stateside that Jericho Industries needs a temporary security force for one of their Libyan business concerns. That's all he knows except that they told him he'd be back home by the end of the week."

Bolan tried to fit what he was hearing into the puzzle.

"So we've got a paid-off general in the States and a covert security force here in Libya," he said. "I think that Jericho has been supplied by Thatcher with something big, has had it transported here, and now he needs his own force to safeguard it. But if Khaddafi is Jericho's buyer, why does Jericho need a civilian outfit with people like Rideout? Why aren't Khaddafi's own forces taking over security?"

Lansdale answered immediately, but there was something of a weariness in his young man's voice.

"Khaddafi is not Jericho's buyer. There is bad blood between Jericho and Khaddafi.

"Remember when Reagan cut off Libyan oil imports to the U.S.? Khaddafi went through the roof. He instigated reprisals at the time against most American interests in Libya. These reprisals never made the world media for a variety of reasons. We still don't know everything that happened. But the Libyan government shut down several U.S. business concerns here, including several that were clearing big profits for Jericho. Three of Jericho's top men in Libya disappeared in the middle of the night and were never heard from again. That was Khaddafi's work and Jericho knows and resents it."

The agent flipped open a folder on his desk and handed a 12x13-inch glossy photograph across to Bolan.

"Here is the man we're fairly certain Jericho is doing business with. Colonel Ahmad Shahkhia. Shahkhia and Khaddafi have been close friends since childhood. Shahkhia is second-in-command, under Khaddafi, of the Libyan army.''

Bolan studied the Arab face in the picture. The photo had evidently been snapped without the colonel's knowledge. Shahkhia was in uniform, sipping from a cup at a sidewalk café. Even from a photograph, in repose, the military commander emanated an aura of forceful ambition. Bolan memorized the face and handed the picture back to Lansdale.

"A coup?"

Lansdale nodded.

"We tumbled to it thanks to our tap on the Russian Embassy in Tripoli."

"I thought Khaddafi was in Moscow's pocket."

"He was and still is, for the time being," said Lansdale. "But that old boy's been getting mighty uppity lately and the Kremlin's looking for a new puppet hereabouts. Shahkhia seems to be it. We've only been onto this since *last night*.

"The conversation we picked up over the embassy line indicates that the Russians are giving Shahkhia the necessary backing and that the coup is set to happen immediately. Shahkhia spoke like someone with a wide base of Libyan support too. Most likely in the military. Considering the timing of Jericho's operation, and Jericho's intense hatred for Khaddafi, I'd say Shahkhia is our best bet as the buyer for whatever Jericho has diverted over here."

"Is Jericho at the villa now?" Bolan's reaction was biased toward action. Enough talk.

"We don't know, Colonel Phoenix. My guess is that the cargo itself is in the possession of this Kennedy guy, the mercenary. His force probably *is* at the villa in Bishabia. Meanwhile Jericho is off somewhere making the final negotiations with Shahkhia, or Shahkhia's people."

"What kind of force does Kennedy have?"

"Paramilitary all the way," said the Company man. "U.S. mercs, mostly. We've not been able to get an accurate manpower count. We do know there have been three or four civilian Huey choppers inside the estate walls of that villa at one time or another recently."

"What happens to the real Mike Rideout?" asked Bolan.

"He'll still be home by the end of the week, just like Jericho's people told him he would," smiled Lansdale.

"One more thing," grunted Bolan. "I must locate a woman, an agent from Puerto Rico, who Jericho is holding prisoner. She's here in Libya with him. Her name is Eve Aguilar."

"Nothing on that, I'm afraid," said Lansdale in his languorous, East Coast prep-school style. "The most I can tell you is that Shahkhia is rumored to have a taste for Western women. Maybe Jericho has something in mind along those lines...."

The two men were only paces from the door. The meeting had come to an end.

"One last thing I guess I should warn you about,"

said Lansdale. "It's something that's been coming through one of the other stations. But we're getting it only one piece at a time. The word is that the Israeli Mossad has already planted an agent of their own in the villa at Bishabia. No connection with us. You have been warned."

Bolan smiled coldly.

"Name of the game," he said, by way of a farewell.

Bolan left the covert complex to rejoin the Benghazi street scene outside. He had a phone call to make. To a man named Kennedy.

Yeah. Libya was definitely booming.

The Executioner was here to make sure it stayed that way.

But with a bigger boom, in the manner of Mack Bolan.

5

They sent a jeep into Benghazi to pick up Bolan at a designated corner in the busy waterfront district.

The jeep driver was a hefty American, outfitted in lightweight desert fatigues, who introduced himself as Doyle, then said no more for the duration of the forty-minute drive from Benghazi.

The adobe-type suburbs thinned out behind them. The jeep rocketed along a sparsely traveled blacktop highway that arrowed south into the rocky wilderness of desert.

The Sahara again.

The harsh wasteland of dunes stretched forever. The land shimmered with waves of heat beneath a bloodred sun. The wind blew in hot, scorching gusts. Thirst came quickly.

Bolan knew from experience that this was a deadly terrain of sand vipers, scorpions and clouds of loathsome flies. The only visible vegetation were the occasional stunted pines or thorny, knee-high shrubs.

It was startling, at one point, to see Arab tents and

a flock of sheep and some camels amid this barren no-man's-land of sand and stone.

An arid land. But to Mack Bolan, a jungle nevertheless.

It was six o'clock.

A mere thirty hours since Mack Bolan's assault on Leonard Jericho's yacht, the *Traveler*, on the other side of the world in Exuma Cay in the Bahamas.

The oasis village of Bishabia was nothing more than a jumble of squalid stone houses and two main dirt streets.

But Leonard Jericho's villa, screened by desert trees beyond the village proper, was in a class by itself.

Doyle wheeled the jeep off the highway and along a winding approach to the front gate.

The walled estate was a blend of Roman and Moorish architecture. Bolan spotted clusters of cedar and aleppo pine trees growing near the outer base of the wall.

The entrance to the grounds was to the west. The concrete wall that surrounded the property was twenty feet high and six inches thick. An iron grille gate barred entrance.

The gate opened mechanically and the jeep passed through. Thus far things were so much easier than breaching Harker's damnable conglomeration in Algeria's Tanezrouft region of this same desert. Grim memories.

A brick gatehouse was situated just inside the wall. A guard, armed with a Galil ARM assault rifle, gave a sharp salute as the jeep rolled past.

Lansdale's intel had been correct. Jericho's security force was paramilitary all the way.

The wrought-iron gates closed automatically behind the jeep. Doyle and "Rideout" drove a short distance into a spacious courtyard at the villa's core.

The core of Lenny Jericho's Something Big.

Three single-engine jet-turbine Bell UHi-D "Huey" helicopters, buff-colored desert models without markings, rested on the pebbled turf of the courtyard. All three choppers were heavily armed, boasting 40mm cannons and 5.56mm miniguns mounted externally on turrets.

Three alert mercs stood guard around one of the aircraft. Other "soldiers" lounged here and there at points around the courtyard, looking hot, oppressed, drenched in sweat.

Bolan made the scene even before the jeep had rolled to a stop. The heavily guarded copter would be carrying whatever cargo it was that Jericho's forces had lifted from the States. The other two Huey gunships would guard the cargo when word came down to rendezvous at a trade-off point with Jericho and Colonel Shahkhia.

The jeep stopped at the front of a flight of marble steps. The opulent-looking steps led up to the entrance of the villa itself.

A man stood waiting, hands on hips, halfway up the wide steps. He was dressed in lightweight fatigues. He had watched the jeep approach. When the vehicle halted, the guy came down the rest of the way with an almost arrogant stride.

This would be Kennedy. Blond-haired, boyish good looks did not fool Bolan. The guy's eyes told the story: the eyes of a killer.

Kennedy carried a 9mm Browning hi-power in a cross-draw position at his left hip. Like those mercs Bolan could see who were not toting Galils, Kennedy also carried a Largo-Star submachine gun strapped over his shoulder.

Bolan knew the Largo as a Spanish copy of the German MP-40, or "Schmeisser." The weapon, referred to by Konzaki back at Stony Man Farm as the Z-45, is fully automatic with a cyclic rate of fire of 550 rounds per minute and a muzzle velocity of some 1,500 fps. Hot stuff.

Kennedy looked at Doyle as Bolan climbed from the jeep.

"Was he wired?"

"Naw, he was clean," reported the driver. "No tails. He's all yours."

"Check out the north wall with Bruner," Kennedy told the driver. "We'll be getting word to pull out any minute now."

Doyle nodded, wheeled the jeep out of sight.

A sweating Kennedy eyeballed Bolan. Bolan eyeballed the honcho right back. Even the long-term pain in his left shoulder from his last overseas mission would not deflect Bolan from meeting iron with iron, which was the way of his new terrorist wars.

"Where the hell you been, Rideout? We coulda been pulled out by now."

"Then I guess I'd have made ten grand the easy way," grunted Bolan in response. "The airlines tied me up. Got here fast as I could."

"I don't like this crap, not knowing who's supposed to be working for me," spat the head cock. "You could be any-damn-body. How do I know you're Mike Rideout?"

"You don't," said Bolan. "So you call it."

Kennedy paused several heartbeats to decide. Few men who ever stood eye to eye with Mack Bolan carried more than a confused and invariably false impression of what the anti-terrorist avenger actually looked like. But there was one detail that never escaped the living memory of a Bolan encounter. And that was the coldly purposeful eyes of the combatman. The Bolan gaze was actually composed of many diverse qualities and could switch from cold death to warm compassion in a flick—or could contain both at one moment. This was not one of those moments. Now it was all cold death. Bolan had the guy psyched and when Kennedy's decision came, Bolan knew that "Mike Rideout" was in.

"Get yourself to the armory in the garage over there," growled the merc. "Arm yourself and suit up. Then go to the southeast corner of this place.

You'll find a guy named Teckert. Tell him I sent you as backup.''

"Sounds like you're expecting something."

"Always expecting, pal. Always ready. We'll be pulling out of here within the hour. Be ready to move.''

6

The rider wore crude shepherd's clothing as a disguise. The gray charger beneath him soared at full gallop across the tumbling landscape of desert wasteland.

Colonel Ahmad Shahkhia pulled rein at the crest of a dune. Below, a stretch of the Benghazi-Jarabub highway arrowed from north to south.

A three-sided tent was pitched against the scorching Sahara sun, some twenty yards off the highway.

One man sat in a camp chair, waiting alone in the tent's shade.

Pornov.

Of course, thought Shahkhia.

The Russian *would* be here early for their meeting. He always was.

Colonel Shahkhia clearly discerned, through the shimmering mirage of afternoon heat, a small bodyguard force, deployed around a cluster of desert vehicles parked another ten yards up the highway from the tent.

The sentries were all heavily armed. Shahkhia spotted rifles, machine guns, a grenade launcher.

The man in shepherd's clothing felt a certain satisfaction at this.

The amount of protection for the general was an indication of their respect for Shahkhia.

And what he was capable of.

Yet, he must be careful. And cautious.

This was a treacherous game he played. Especially now.

Shahkhia fully understood that success, at this point, rested solely on his maintaining a confident facade to all involved in the unfolding drama.

The rider spurred his mount into a sideways canter along the face of the sloping dune.

Shahkhia wondered why the Russian had contacted him for a meeting. This was not a time that Colonel Shahkhia wished to be seen making contact with anyone who might cast the slightest hint of suspicion on him, most notably the Russians. Most notably on this day of days.

Nothing would stop Colonel Shahkhia from keeping his rendezvous this evening with Leonard Jericho.

Nothing!

Shahkhia realized once again exactly how dangerous was this game he played with Pornov, the KGB agent from Moscow.

Be very cautious, the rider reminded himself again as Pornov's tent grew closer. Do not make the same mistakes in dealing with these people who are about to bring down Moammar.

Brother Colonel Khaddafi was one year older than Ahmad Shahkhia's own thirty-seven years. They were of the same tribe, and it seemed to Shahkhia that he had always been forced, by circumstance, to live in Moammar's shadow.

Shahkhia had been aware of this from their very earliest days together. And he had *always* resented it. And always waited for the day when he, Ahmad Shahkhia, could step from the Khadaffi shadow and claim the ruling power of Libya as his own. It was his destiny, he would tell himself. His fate. He deserved no less. And now...yes, now the time had come. Shahkhia's visions of a lifetime were about to become reality.

Ahmad Shahkhia knew that he would not make the same mistakes as Khaddafi.

While in Moammar's shadow, Ahmad had observed and studied very closely, and he felt that he had learned his lessons well.

He had even been with Khaddafi when the two men attended Britain's Sandhurst military college together, the only time in his life when Ahmad had ever been away from his beloved desert. The young men had walked about London in their traditional Bedouin robes, causing all manner of sensation at a time when such an act was considered an Arab defiance of the West. And, indeed, it was *exactly* that!

Ahmad Shahkhia and Moammar Khaddafi had been lowly captains together in the Libyan army when Khaddafi commanded his efficient bloodless military coup against Libya's Western-backed monarch, King Idris, while the eighty-year-old monarch was out of the country in 1969.

The country belonged to Moammar then.

Khaddafi became, now and forever, Brother Colonel, the all powerful leader of his people; the invincible agent of Allah's will on earth.

And jealousy ate at Ahmad's guts like a spreading cancer.

Precious oil beneath the Sahara sand became the key to a power far greater than anything imagined by either Shahkhia or Khaddafi.

The Soviet Union needed oil for survival as much as the West did. And Moscow was willing to offer far more than the petrodollars of the capitalists.

Russia rapidly became Libya's principal arms supplier.

Oil deals with the USSR had allowed Khaddafi's military to acquire more than $10 billion worth of highly sophisticated Soviet weaponry.

But always, with the weapons. . . came conditions.

Khaddafi—and Shahkhia—knew that Libya was expected by the Kremlin to supply the fist behind Soviet expansion in Africa.

Still, such a role could only lead to more power.

Khaddafi was happy to oblige.

Colonel Ahmad Shahkhia shared in the power. But

always—always!—awaiting his chance to step out from Khaddafi's shadow.

Ahmad was careful to mask his ambition. He bided his time.

Two months ago, his waiting paid off.

He had been discreetly approached by General Pornov, of the Russian Embassy in Tripoli.

For some time now, it was explained by General Pornov, Brother Colonel Khaddafi had become increasingly too "ambitious." For ambitious, read crazy.

Pornov had not elaborated, but implied that the Kremlin was far from pleased. It was past time for a change. They were scouting for someone new to take Khaddafi's place, fast. Someone who would be more... appreciative, more *stable*.

Someone like Colonel Shahkhia.

A deal was struck. Ahmad would plan and lead a coup to overthrow Khaddafi.

Pornov would supply the weaponry and financing needed to launch such a military overthrow.

It was set to happen in two days. All was in readiness. The plan, to Shahkhia's mind, was perfect. Shahkhia had given arms to members of rogue Bedouin tribes who roamed the desert. The tribesmen would do the dirty work, attacking key military installations around the country that had been carefully selected by Ahmad and his fellow plotters. Well-coordinated attacks by the Bedouins would weaken Khaddafi politically as well as militarily.

Brother Colonel would be disgraced, seen as a leader too weak to control civil disorder.

Troops loyal to Colonel Shahkhia would then march in and restore order from chaos. And of course the tribesmen would be duly paid for their work, clandestinely.

Yes, only two days. . . and Ahmad Shahkhia would never again stand in another man's shadow.

But why had Pornov issued this summons to a meeting in the center of nowhere? There was no traffic whatsoever along this stretch of desert highway. Only the sand, the Russians and the line of telephone poles and wire, reaching from horizon to horizon.

The uniformed Russian KGB man stood at the very edge of the tent's shade. He was waiting for the approaching rider.

Pornov was squat, oxlike. To Shahkhia, the Russian pig farmer always seemed to be slick with perspiration in his confining brown uniform.

The "shepherd" pulled rein short yards from the tent, dismounted and approached the KGB man. The Russian spoke in clipped English as the two men exchanged a handshake. English was the only language known to them both.

"Colonel Shahkhia, I am glad you were able to keep our appointment."

There was a smugness in the Russian's voice that was vaguely unsettling.

"General Pornov." Ahmad noticed that the general's camp chair was the only furniture in the small tent. The Russian and the Arab remained standing. "I trust there have been no complications in our arrangements."

"Not from our end," said Pornov. His small eyes glittered like polished beads. "But complications, yes. It seems, my dear Colonel, that you have underestimated myself and the people I represent."

Shahkhia felt cool fingers of fear caress his spine.

"Underestimate you? How?"

"Fool!" snapped Pornov. "You deal with others. You are to meet the American, Leonard Jericho, this evening at the army base at Aujila, to close a deal you have made with him without my sanction."

Shahkhia prayed that he was not showing outwardly the rising panic he felt inside.

"My General, you must be mistaken—"

Even to Ahmad, the voice did not sound like his own.

"I am not mistaken," said Pornov icily. "It need not concern you how I came by this information. I believe that two words will suffice to persuade you, Colonel Shahkhia, that I do know of what I speak. The two words. . . .*Strain-7*."

"General Pornov, I'm sure there has been some mistake—"

"There most certainly has, Colonel! And it has been made by you. I fear you forget the power I hold over your conniving head. One telephone call to the office of Brother Colonel and that head will roll."

"We are coconspirators, General Pornov."

"Obviously I will deny any allegations you make against the Russian Embassy, and do you know? Colonel Khaddafi could not afford to disbelieve me!"

Shahkhia felt his throat go as dry as the desert sand on which they stood.

"My General, I had planned to turn over the consignment to you, once it was mine."

"Do not lie to me, Shahkhia."

"The man called Jericho would not deal with the Soviet Union," insisted the Arab. "And I thought something so important should be obtained for our cause."

"You thought only of your own ambition," snarled Pornov. "You thought of the power that would be yours. You will keep your scheduled rendezvous with Mr. Jericho. I will accompany you. And you may thank your beloved Allah that your life has been spared. My people will contact you later today regarding flight plans for tonight. That is all."

Pornov spun around and strode back toward his cluster of men and vehicles with the stiff military bearing of the parade field.

The Libyan officer mounted his steed. He whipped the horse into a gallop, retracing his approach already obliterated by the shifting sands.

Colonel Shahkhia did not look back.

As the rider in shepherd's clothing, and the gray charger beneath him, topped the dune and put the scene of the confrontation behind, Colonel Ahmad Shahkhia exerted all of his self-control at calming a mind still in turmoil from the scene with the Russian.

Shahkhia understood that it might become necessary to kill Pornov. This would be a most delicate matter, indeed. But Ahmad Shahkhia would *not* be stopped. Not this close to attaining all of his lifelong dreams. When he obtained what Jericho now had, the power would truly be his.

Nothing shall stop me, thought Shahkhia, except Death itself. It would take a mighty executioner to get *his* head to roll.

There was another element to consider in addition to Pornov; an occurrence, mentioned in Leonard Jericho's last communiqué to Shahkhia, that Pornov seemed not to be aware of.

The coded communiqué had carried vague reference to an attack on a yacht owned by Jericho in the Bahamas. It was the vessel aboard which the American end of this operation had been initiated.

Jericho's representatives had finalized the arrangement with the American general, Thatcher. The shipment had immediately left ground at Houston International Airport in Texas, America, and was now in Libya, according to Jericho. Along with the "gift" Jericho had promised.

The human gift.

A woman.

But what of the assault on Leonard Jericho's

yacht? Was it related to Shahkhia's business with Jericho?

Colonel Shahkhia felt a premonition.

It gave him a creepier feeling even than the knowledge of General Pornov's damnably correct Intelligence.

Only thoughts of Jericho's flesh gift could relieve his queasiness. Yes, having his way with her would be of supreme interest. How thoughtful of Jericho to feed his tireless appetite for the unusual....

Thoughtful enough to earn him Shahkhia's alliance. So a curse on this nefarious attack on the other side of the globe. What foul surprise would beset them all next?

7

The temporary command post for the mission was an office barrack at the north end of the courtyard of Jericho's villa.

The low building was equipped to function as base headquarters for Lenny Jericho's far-flung operation whenever the big man stayed there.

The building was deserted now except for the quarters that were Kennedy's office and orderly room.

The topkick merc stood at the window that faced north from the villa. He watched the sky fade from deep purple into night as the sun disappeared behind the rocky silhouette of the Jebel el Akdar mountain range.

The hot Sahara winds of daytime had already died down. The temperature would now drop abruptly into the mid-fifties.

Kennedy understood the desert very well. The love of his life was soldiering, and this was his seventh assignment in North Africa. Yes, he knew the desert. He knew it and he hated it.

After tonight, he thought, I'll never walk on sand again.

He glanced at his watch. He wondered when he would be hearing from Leonard Jericho. He was tired of waiting.

Doyle was in the office with Kennedy. Doyle was second in the chain of command on this mission. Right now he appeared to read Kennedy's mind.

"The call should have come by now, don'cha think, Top? The men are starting to get restless."

Kennedy turned impatiently from the window.

"They're paid to hurry up and wait, and they know that. Tell 'em to stow it. We'll be lifting off soon enough. I got other things on my mind."

"Such as?"

"That new guy."

"Rideout?"

"What'd you think of him, Doyle?"

The second-in-command lit a cigarette thoughtfully. "Funny you should mention the guy. I've been thinking about him too."

"Like, what?" asked Kennedy. "You drove him out here from Benghazi. Did he talk much?"

"Like a clam. So what's with this job anyway?"

"Knock off the questions," growled the topkick. "The headshed screwed it up, as usual. I don't like it either. But we work with what we got."

Doyle got thoughtful again.

"If we're talking about Rideout, I don't know what we got, exactly. I couldn't read the guy worth a damn. There's something about him. It's in the eyes.

Cold eyes, Top, like chips of blue ice. The guy looks like he can handle himself.''

"Maybe that's it," nodded Kennedy. "He's *too* cool. Showing up here late. And looking like he's got ice in his veins.''

"I thought that was the kind of man we wanted here. What is it? You got a gut feeling about the guy?''

"Maybe. I don't know. I got a gut feeling that the guy's a pro all right. But not the kind of pro we want. I got the feeling I was being *handled* out there when I met him.''

Doyle eyeballed Kennedy keenly.

"So what do we do about him? Jericho might not like it if we don't have proof.''

"We'll give Jericho the next best thing, if I'm right,'' grunted Kennedy. "What have you got on the other thing?''

"I think we got what you wanted,'' replied Doyle. "It was the guy you had tagged, just like you said. I had two men on his ass and they took him right to the doorstep of a woman we know works for Mossad.''

"Your men should've dusted him right on the spot and those others with him,'' grunted Kennedy. He was pacing the office floor restlessly. "Now we've got to deal with him here. Tonight.''

"My men didn't know they were trailing an Israeli spy,'' Doyle bristled mildly. "Those were your orders.''

Kennedy suddenly snapped his fingers, stopped pacing.

"Wait a minute. There's a way we can tie these two things together."

"I don't get you, Top."

Which is why you'll always be a dumb ass kisser and nothing more, thought Kennedy. His response was interrupted by the shrill ring of the phone on the office desk.

"Here come the orders," said Doyle.

Kennedy palmed the receiver.

"Yes?" was all he said.

"Relax," a voice said. "I've got a scrambler on the line. How are things going there?"

The question was asked in an authoritative tone that made it anything but polite conversation.

"My men are ready and waiting to move out, Mr. Jericho," said Kennedy crisply. "Waiting on orders from you."

"Very good. What about our Israeli problem?"

"We've got the man tagged, sir. I'm making plans right now to take him out."

"Good. About goddamn time. New developments?"

Kennedy was aware that Doyle eyed him closely from across the office. But Kennedy saw no reason to bring up his suspicions concerning Mike Rideout. Kennedy would deal with Rideout at his level.

"No, sir. Nothing new. I've got security airtight. It's all running good like I said it would."

"Then set a course for the Aujila oasis. That's

about thirty minutes flying time. Be there in one hour."

Kennedy glanced at his watch.

Perfect, he thought.

"One hour. Yes, sir. I'll brief the pilots immediately."

"I will see you in one hour then, Mr. Kennedy."

"Yes, sir. Goodbye, sir."

Kennedy replaced the receiver. He turned to confront the open question marks in Doyle's eyes.

"Aujila oasis," Kennedy told him. "Keep everyone at their post for right now. We'll have a quick pull out in twenty minutes."

Doyle was on his feet. He started from the office, but paused with his hand on the doorknob.

"You didn't say anything about Rideout."

Kennedy's eyes narrowed. "You haven't figured it out yet?"

"I guess I have," said Doyle. "I'll set that up too, then."

Kennedy nodded.

"Use Bruner and Teckert. Tell them to watch their asses. I got that damn *feeling*."

"I wonder if we're right. About Rideout, I mean."

"Either way we'll find out soon enough."

"You want it, you got it," said Doyle. He snapped off a curt salute and left the office, closing the door behind him.

Leaving Kennedy alone to his thoughts.

The boss merc turned to stare out the window. It

was too dark to see anything out there except his own reflection in the glass. But it would give Doyle a few minutes in case the guy came back with any last-minute questions. It would do no good for Doyle to return and find Kennedy gone, with no one having seen him emerge from the office out front. That would not do at all.

I've got to be real careful now, thought Kennedy. This damn thing has been like walking on eggs. But these final minutes are crucial. . . .

The world looked at Kennedy and saw unlined, youthful features that he knew were attractive to most of the women he came in contact with. His eyes sparkled. His smile could dazzle.

In other words, the horrors that he had perpetrated, and the hellzones—Vietnam, Nicaragua, El Salvador, Rhodesia, Chad, Libya—where he had spent his career soldiering amid the harsh realities of a world he never made, could not be imagined from his outward appearance.

Kennedy was willing to concede that a few people over the years might have guessed at the true limits of behavior that he was capable of, but not many.

Even some of the men in his outfit here in Bishabia would be shocked to know about the locked and boarded schoolhouse full of rebel kids near Gatooma that Kennedy had burned to the ground some years ago. The job had been on orders, sure, but some of the mercs here tonight would damn sure have blanched at a thing like that and refused—because they never had Kennedy's ambition and drive—to do *anything* that would establish him as the toughest, baddest, *best* merc in the business. It was too bad about those kids in Gatooma. It was too bad about a lot of things. But no, it was not a world that Kennedy had made, to his way of thinking. It was a world that he was trying to get ahead in. To accomplish that, you needed ambition and drive and the knowledge that winning was everything.

It worked for Kennedy. It got him qualified enough to honcho a mission like this for no less a VIP than Mr. Leonard Jericho himself.

Kennedy smiled at the reflection in the dark glass.

Yes, it worked and here you are. You're sitting on a cargo worth enough to get you into a life of comfort forever.

Enough time had passed.

Kennedy stalked across the office and locked the door from the inside. Then he went directly toward what appeared to be a bare niche in one wall.

He was thinking that there was one man, a newcomer, here tonight who might understand the truth about what kind of a man Kennedy really was. If such was indeed the case, then that man might have ideas of his own. The thought did not sit well with the boss merc.

Kennedy stepped up to the niche in the wall, then stooped down and used his right-hand thumb to press on a part of the floorboard where wall met floor.

The wall section slid sideways to reveal a steep, narrow flight of stairs.

Movie stuff, smiled Kennedy.

The wall slid noiselessly back into place behind him. Kennedy briskly continued down the stairs.

He was thinking about the big, quiet man with the steely blue eyes.

Kennedy knew that a direct confrontation between himself and Michael Rideout could only end in death. They were equals with regards to capabilities. The big man had a look of deadly competence, the quiet look of a true hellgrounder.

Kennedy had convinced himself that "Rideout" was not the guy's real name. And that a confrontation with the big guy was somehow inevitable. It was coming soon.

Tonight.

Along with everything else.

8

Mack Bolan, on combat duty in Vietnam, led his Penetration Able Team on many successful classified missions behind enemy lines. Bolan was a penetration specialist, a penetration master.

That was how he appreciated immediately, by taking position in the background from where a soft surveillance could be maintained, the interesting information that security at the Jericho villa in Bishabia was *very* tight.

The Executioner felt a respect for Kennedy in the manner in which Jericho's top merc had deployed his manpower to guard this villa. Subliminal quivers in the psyche called Bolan to quick-pass a number of emplacements that were planned to bite inward as well as out. This was the whole nine yards here. It tickled something in his combat instinct, he felt the tremor of the game now.

The death look they wore indicated that the soldiers in this base were lethal even if they were also non-notable, the wolf pack fit to devour at any moment, savages in every respect.

After he outfitted himself in the armory in desert

camouflage fatigues, and armed himself with a Galil, some grenades and a holstered Browning hi-power, Bolan made his way across the villa's courtyard, past the Hueys and up the tall ladder to the parapet, toward the villa's southeast corner. Mike Rideout was obediently following Kennedy's orders.

Bolan eyed Kennedy's heavily armed troops as he did so. In addition to a few AK-47s, Galils and Largos, he also noted several new Beretta Model 70 assault rifles that Bolan knew to be capable of spitting out 5.56mm death-dealers at a blistering 700 rpm.

Some of the mercs wore munitions belts heavy with grenades. Two men seen by Bolan wore .357's on their hips Western-style, the way Bolan now wore his Browning hi-power.

The only other small arms he could see were several SIG 9mm Parabellum P210 autos. Some of the mercs carried these in underarm shoulder holsters.

"Rideout" had drawn duty with a U.S. merc named Teckert, who sat perched behind a belt-fed Cartouche light machine gun, tripod-rigged atop the wall's ledge. A sheet held up by four posts protected each of these gun posts from the sun.

Teckert was a man of few words.

So was Bolan.

They got along fine.

Nothing moved beyond the villa walls. Utter stillness reigned.

At one point a Swede merc named Hohlstrom came along the parapet. Teckert introduced Hohlstrom to Bolan. Hohlstrom barely nodded. His eyes were dark marbles. His expressionless face was hard beneath a high intellectual brow and a pate of thinning hair.

Hohlstrom said nothing to Bolan.

Hohlstrom and Doyle exchanged grunted monosyllables, then Hohlstrom lumbered on. This was a world where a man kept his counsel unless he knew well the man to whom he was speaking.

A few minutes later another merc approached along the parapet. Apparently, Kennedy had roving sentries in addition to those at set stations, like Teckert and Rideout.

This merc was a German national named Bruner. Teckert and Bruner knew each other; there was a brief, low-keyed exchange between the two mercs as Bolan eavesdropped.

"So what do you think of this scene, Teckert? Easy money so far?"

"So far."

"Reminds me of the time we took Brother Khaddafi's wages at Aozou in Chad. Remember?"

Teckert spat over the wall.

"I remember. I hate these frigging desert jobs."

"But do you remember the women of Aozou?" prodded Bruner with a guttural laugh.

Teckert grunted. "Yeah, I remember. Too bad we had to torch that village."

Bruner snorted. "You should not *think*, my friend."

And he moved on.

Yeah, thought Bolan. These are the bad ones. These are the purest enemy.

Don't think, huh? Very soon, Mack Bolan was going to force them to think, even though it would be their last lesson.

He was going to teach them an essential paradox of warfare. He was going to show them that men are never more in danger than when they believe themselves secure.

And that they—or rather he, Mack Bolan—would never be more secure than when in the very greatest danger.

That required some thought. Mack Bolan's kind of thinking.

"Be right back," grunted Bolan to Teckert. "Time for a pitstop."

Bolan ambled off toward a nearby ladder leading down from the parapet.

Teckert said nothing to stop him. He continued gazing out from behind the Cartouche machine gun at the dark wasteland beyond the villa walls.

Bolan kept his easy pace until he had climbed the ladder to a point out of Teckert's line of vision. Once he could not be seen, Bolan moved with speed and economy of movement.

Even in the light-hued desert camo fatigues, Mack Bolan was a wraith in the darkness as he descended to the base of the wall. He carried the Browning and, on its strap over his shoulder, the Galil assault rifle.

This corner of the villa was removed from the hubbub in the courtyard. Bolan found himself in mottled shadows. He melded with the lighter shades, reversing the tactic he used with his skintight combat blacks. His movements were of silence and cunning, pure stealth in the pale night.

He strode along the far end of the courtyard, toward what looked like the main residence.

He turned right at a generator shack that was feeding power to Jericho's villa.

It would have been a pleasure to plant some plastique in the generator shed. But Mike Rideout was not in a position to be carrying that kind of material.

Bolan moved on, angling toward the part-time residence of Leonard Jericho.

Bolan figured the odds were as good as not that Eve was being held in this villa outside Bishabia. Therefore an intel probe was required.

He cut into the shadows under a stone arch. He was near a side door to the private residence. He could see a faint light glowing from a window along the wall.

Bolan tried the door handle. The door was unlocked, as he had expected it to be. Security around here came from guns, not locks. What could not be contained by heavy guard deserved to be trapped into temptation.

Bolan slipped soundlessly into a darkened foyer.

His every sense was alert as if to sniff out a trap. The only light in the hallway was a rectangle of illumination midway down the corridor, coming from a half-open door that corresponded with the light Bolan had seen from the outside.

He closed the door behind him, then unlimbered the Browning hi-power from its hip holster. Bolan kept to the wall and moved toward the lighted doorway.

When he was three feet from the doorway, he heard sounds.

A man, a Libyan outfitted in servant's attire, emerged from the room at a leisurely pace. He was still munching the remnants of a sandwich.

The servant saw Bolan. His eyes and mouth widened in alarm.

Bolan stepped forward and chopped the guy hard with a downward snap of the Browning's butt. The step and the chop were one and the same movement. The blow connected at the base of the man's neck.

The Libyan fell to his knees. His eyes rolled back in his head as he pitched forward onto the floor. He did not move. His breathing was an uncertain rattle. He would be out for at least half an hour.

Bolan frisked him. The guy was unarmed. So Bolan would not kill him.

The Executioner grabbed the unconscious figure under both arms. He dragged the servant back to a walk-in closet next to the door. He laid him out on the floor of the closet, then closed the door and walked on.

It took him all of eight minutes to give the sprawling two-story residence a thorough search.

Lenny Jericho was a man who apparently lived in luxury wherever he went. His home in the desert was a living museum of exquisite tapestries, rugs and furniture in various Mediterranean and African styles.

Evidently the servant was the only one home.

There was no sign of Eve Aguilar. There was no sign of any part of the house being used as a place of detention.

Damnation.

Bolan exited the house by the same open door near the unconscious servant.

He hoped that Teckert would assume by now that Rideout had been assigned some other duty during his time below the parapet.

He kept to the shadows and eased out from the corner of the private residence to the rear wall of a one-story building that formed part of the villa's square courtyard.

Bolan's finger stayed curled around the trigger of the Browning hi-power. His senses scanned the darkness around him as he stayed close to the wall, stealthily moving toward another single lighted window.

He bent his knees slightly when he reached it, and edged an eye to the lower corner of the window. He looked in.

The room was an office.

Kennedy and Doyle stood near the office doorway. They were earnestly discussing something that Bolan could not hear. The windows had been double-glazed to facilitate the air conditioning.

Bolan watched.

Doyle snapped a curt salute at Kennedy. The subordinate left the office. When the door was closed, Kennedy turned and crossed over to the window through which Bolan was looking.

Bolan ducked down out of sight. He took care to prevent the barrel of the Galil from poking out over his shoulder.

As he crouched against the cool brick of the building and looked up, he had a good chance to study Kennedy's features.

The merc honcho stared out above him into the blackness.

It looked to Bolan as if Kennedy had plenty on his mind. The merc's too-perfect good looks were intact and unruffled. But Bolan was close enough to see that Kennedy's eyes were not as clear as before. They were heavy lidded, as if important matters were weighing on Kennedy's mind.

Close to two minutes passed before Kennedy turned from the window. Then Bolan took another chance and peered into the room.

Kennedy was locking the office door. Bolan watched him cross to an empty niche in the wall across from the window.

Then Kennedy stooped and pressed the floorboard. The wall slid open.

The head merc stepped briskly into a secret passage. The sliding panel closed shut behind him.

Now what was this?

Bolan straightened from his crouch. He tried the window. It was latched shut.

He used his elbow to tap it with just enough strength to crack the glass, not enough to shatter it. He pressed his fingertips along the crack in the glass. It gave way and fell onto the sill inside, with nothing more than a soft, dull thud.

Bolan reached in with his free hand and swiftly unlatched the window. He pushed the window up, then swung his leg up and over the window ledge, fanning the interior with his eyes and pistol.

It was not a trap.

The office was empty.

Bolan strode without hesitation toward the bare niche in the wall.

The Executioner was going after Kennedy, who would take him to Eve Aguilar.

Before it was too late.

9

Bolan pressed the floorboard.

The wall panel slid open—powered by some soundless automatic mechanism—exactly as it had for Kennedy.

Bolan's pistol was raised and ready for anything that might come out at him. He moved into the opening. He was one and a half minutes behind Kennedy. The panel slid back into place behind him.

He was enveloped in silence.

Low-watt light bulbs were evenly spaced down the angled ceiling of a narrow stairway. At the bottom, the stairway fed into a corridor that bisected the house from Bolan's left to right.

He eased down the stairs toward the shadows at its base. The air was dead and cold. It penetrated his bones.

He could hear nothing.

The man he was tracking seemed to be long gone. Seemed to be.

When he reached the second-from-the-bottom stair, Bolan paused again, his pistol up. He stole a look around the corner of the stone wall.

He could see no beginning nor end to the tunnel that stretched away in either direction.

More light bulbs had been installed here, but long distances apart so that patches of stygian gloom gave the passageway an eerie, menacing reality.

Bolan slid around the corner and kept low. He started off down the tunnel to his right.

A cool but barely discernible draft brushed the hairs on his arms. It originated from far up ahead.

He held the slung Galil assault rifle in close against his body to prevent noise from the weapon bouncing against him.

The curved stone ceiling of the passage barely accommodated his 6%3* height. After several hundred yards, the tunnel made a sharp incline. Deeper still.

Then Bolan saw light, faint light, coming from the cracks of an ill-fitting door some ten yards ahead. Surely this was the source of the moving air he had noticed.

He pressed himself against the curving stone of the tunnel. He paused when he was still several feet from the door. He listened intently. There was a room of some sort beyond that wooden door, but it would be empty—Bolan heard no sounds from within. Or... it could be a trap.

He stood against the wall at the very edge of the doorframe. He extended his right foot and gave the door a slight nudge. The door was unlatched. It swung inward.

Bolan looked inside cautiously. The Browning hi-power panned the room, simultaneously with his eyes.

The floor was earthen. It was a storage room, with a door on the opposite wall. A candle emitted the light that had drawn Bolan.

Two people were in the room. Libyan civilians: an old man and a young woman. They were tied to kitchen chairs. Tied and gagged. They were alone in the room. Their eyes watched with puzzlement—and fear—as Bolan stepped toward them.

The man could have been fifty or a hundred years old. He wore a dark robe and white headcloth. The snowy white of his beard was in stark contrast to the dark of his Arabian skin.

The woman was a girl. Bolan judged her to be sixteen, if that. But she was already budding with the sensual-eyed, lush beauty that Bolan knew to be the birthright of the sisterhood of Islam.

He ungagged the girl, then the man.

The girl was fooled by the leathery brown of Bolan's skin hue, which had been acquired over an adulthood of missions to every hotspot under the sun.

She chattered at Bolan in Arabic.

Bolan stepped back. He cautioned her to lower her voice with a waved hand.

"Do you speak English?" he whispered.

"I do. Some," replied the girl quietly. "Who are you?"

"A friend. Tell me why you're here."

"This is our home. My father manages the inn of the village."

Bolan made his decision. He undid the ropes that bound them to the chairs.

"I'm looking for Kennedy." In a hushed voice he described the boss merc to her. "Did he come through here? Do you know where he went?"

The old man muttered something in Arabic. The only word Bolan could make out was "Kennedy."

"He is an evil man," said the girl. She rubbed the burn marks where the rope had chafed her wrists. "At first we thought he was from the villa."

"What are your names?" whispered Bolan. "Tell me what happened here. Quickly."

"I am called Fahima," she said. "This is my father, Bushir. The man you call Kennedy, he has kept us like this for two days now. He keeps us alive in case the owner of the villa should try to contact us."

"What is your employer's name?"

"We have never met him," said Fahima. "He is with an oil company. A Mr. Conrad. An American. A solicitor in Benghazi. He also owns the villa."

"His real name is Jericho," grunted Bolan under his breath. "Has he used this escape route often?"

"Once. Khaddafi's troops were in the area, searching for him." At the word *Khaddafi*, the old man began prattling angrily. "My family was dispossessed during the land reform," explained Fahima. "We are willing to help Mr. Conrad against a common enemy."

"You must trust me," said Bolan. "I'm getting you and your father out of this place. There's going to be killing here tonight. Do you know where Kennedy has gone?"

"He is in the building above. They closed the inn two days ago. We can hear them sometimes. I heard footsteps earlier tonight."

"Where in your inn would be a good place for a secret meeting?"

The girl thought for a moment. "One of two places. There is a dining room away from the lobby, as you approach from the corridor outside. And there is a private room on the floor above that."

"How many men does Kennedy have with him?"

"Only one, I believe. A guard on the door." She pointed at the door opposite to where Bolan had entered. It was massive, most likely of imported oak. Beyond it would be a route into the inn above.

"One last question," whispered Bolan. "Did Kennedy bring a woman with him?"

Fahima shook her head. "No woman. No one. Only the one you call Kennedy, and the man outside."

Bolan started toward the door.

"Let's go," he muttered to the man and his daughter. "Keep low. Do as I say. When you see a chance, run for the nearest cover."

Fahima studied him with soulful, unblinking eyes.

"I understand," she said. She had a surprisingly gentle voice. "You are a brave man for helping us."

The Executioner yanked the heavy door open with one hand, gripping his Browning hi-power in the other.

The Bolan Effect had arrived.

Fahima Dohmi watched the big American as he prepared to dispatch to oblivion the sentry in the corridor, who stood with his back to the doorway.

Fahima thought that she had never seen a man move with such grace and determination as the big American. He radiated animal ferocity and strength worthy of a son of the desert.

She had watched as he pulled the door recklessly open.

Now she saw the sentry spin around, reaching for a side arm.

She saw the American warrior grab the sentry around the throat with his forearm before the guard could complete his turn.

A quick snap punch to the temple with a raised pistol and the man slumped to the floor, his skull cracked. She saw blood dribble from one ear.

The big man led the way out of the room, stepping across the corpse that blocked the doorway.

Like a son of the desert, she thought again.

Bolan heard movement from around a corner in the hallway. He motioned a halt.

Fahima and Bushir froze in their tracks. It was too late for any of them to backtrack now.

Three men came around the corner. They were heavyset black men in African military uniforms.

Bolan could not identify their political origin in the instant that eyeball recognition was made on both sides.

The three Africans toted AK-47s by slung shoulder straps. The troopers had evidently been headed toward the room where the father and daughter had been held. There was purpose in their marching stride.

When they saw Bolan and the others, the three of them registered identical surprise. They fell away from each other and fought to sling their weapons around in a race for survival. The movements provoked grunts, a curse.

The pistol in Bolan's fist chugged a death cough. Hot millimeters of parabellum lead lanced through space.

The soldier on Bolan's left caught a round that smashed his head sharply backward against the wall, splashing the wall with bloody brains. The dead cock slid down the wall into a heap, the AK spilling useless alongside him.

Of the other two soldiers, the one directly before Bolan was the immediate threat. The trooper's big hands guided his rifle into a smooth underhand arc, pulling aim on Bolan.

The Browning had already spat. Twice this time. Two head shots. The soldier never completed target acquisition. He was kicked instead into Infinity in a backward halo of exploding head.

Bolan crouched and twisted, one movement, as he

swung the kill piece around and at the lone remaining soldier.

This last soldier had a firm grip on his AK. He too was bringing it around with commendable speed toward Bolan.

The soldier's movement was halted by a whirling short-bladed knife that whistled through the air to Bolan's right. It embedded itself to the hilt in the soldier's throat.

The man gagged frantically, released the rifle, started to grab his ravaged throat. Blood bubbled from the mouth. The knees buckled. The corpse collapsed to the floor.

"Allah wa-akbar!" intoned old Bushir.

A ubiquitous Muslim phrase that Bolan recognized. God is great. Yeah. Bolan understood that.

Fahima's father had pulled the military knife from the equipment belt of the dead sentry who had been the first to die. Mack Bolan need not have purchased his.

Bolan flashed an appreciative smile. The old man returned it.

The Executioner led the two Libyans along the hallway toward a doorway leading outside.

The killing here had only just begun.

10

The nightfighter palmed a fresh clip into the Browning. He unscrewed the low-watt bulb near the door. The hallway bisected the stone building. There had been noise tonight, from the Browning. But security at this level, deep beneath a secret meeting place, was spacious—sparse and unassuming like a secret itself.

At the opposite end, stairs led up to the main room of the structure where Bolan would find his primary targets. His concern, too, was to get Fahima and Bushir out of the killing zone.

Bolan inched the door inward a few inches. He scanned the narrow, rutted dirt street outside the doorway.

The scene was deserted, cloaked in darkness. The village of Bishabia dozed beneath the desert night.

Bolan could sense the tension of the father and daughter who stood close behind him.

He also sensed an electricity out there in the night. There was a crackle to the air. Bolan knew in his gut that others were roaming. On the kill. He did not know how many or who. But they were there.

He holstered the Browning and spun the Galil into readiness. He toed the door further open and stepped into the night like a shadow. A shadow in combat crouch.

He surveyed the scene: he saw nothing but the night.

"Move along the wall away from me," commanded Bolan over his shoulder to Fahima and her father. "When we get to the end of the building, you're on your own. Good luck."

They exited the building and did as they were told. Bolan covered them from the rear.

They almost made it.

The crunch of several pairs of footsteps came from around the corner of the building when Bolan's group was less than two yards from it.

Four of Jericho's free-lance terrorist troopers, black and burly and uniformed like the men Bolan had killed inside, came into sight at a leisurely clip.

Everyone saw everybody else at the same instant.

Bushir and his daughter knew they would only be in Bolan's way. Father and daughter went low, wisely falling away from the hellground that would be the airspace above. Bushir moved with an agility surprising for a man his age.

Bolan was diving into a prone firing position. The rifle was right for night killing like this.

He pumped off two rounds, was rewarded with the sight of one soldier flopping back, open armed, as if kicked by a mule.

The Galil's report echoed like a thundercrack in the tight confines of the village street.

The soldiers were scattering. They appeared untrained. But they were pulling their weapons around fast enough.

Bolan sighted in on one guy dodging to the side. The Galil pumped two more lead destroyers that flipped the man into a forward somersault, minus his face.

The two survivors had held flank positions in their original formation. Both men opened fire with their rifles. But they could not see Bolan. They were firing at where they thought he was.

Saffron flashes of gunfire knifed the darkness.

Bolan was rolling in a sideways fling, wide and wild to his left. He heard bullets chunking into the dirt where he had been moments before.

He came out of the roll, sighted at the man to his left and squeezed the trigger. The guy jackknifed with an ugly grunt and pitched to the ground. Bolan had heard clearly the *thwack-suck* as the heavy round splattered through living matter. That soldier was dead.

The remaining man of the group tossed a fast trio of parting shots and started to turn.

Bolan heard a gasping noise to his right. He concentrated immediately on taking out the soldier who was two paces from gaining cover at the corner of the building.

The assault rifle thumped once, twice more. The

target was twisted around and slammed into the corner of the building he had been trying to hide behind. His corpse slumped slowly to the ground. Bolan had heard those hits, too. The guy was dead.

The night was responding with a hum of activity. The babble of awakened villagers merged with something else.

Bolan heard two separate engines gunning to life. He heard voices raised in alarm. He heard the sound of men mobilizing.

Bolan hurried to where Fahima knelt beside the body of her father.

Bushir had caught one high in the chest. The old man had not been quite agile enough. He was sprawled onto his back with a gaping, pulpy hole above his heart that still pumped blood. His legs extended straight, his arms were flung out. He looked like a man crucified. He was dead.

Fahima was wringing her father's hand. She was in anguish, wailing in Arabic.

Bolan stooped, placed an arm around the young woman, and gently yet forcefully guided her to her feet.

"Fahima. Listen to me. You must run. Get away from here."

"My father!" she cried. Her features were twisted. "He's all I have.... They've killed him...."

He slapped her gently, but sharply.

She snapped to attention, hysteria forgotten.

"You can come back," he pressed. "But stay now

and you'll be killed. Get away from here, Fahima. It's me they want. I'll engage them. You git. *Now!*"

He did not wait for her response. He turned and stalked back toward the rear entrance of the inn. He held the Galil with a finger on the trigger, his eyes constantly probing.

He heard soft words, carried on the night wind. Fahima's woman-child voice:

"Thank you, American. May Allah protect you."

He sensed Fahima moving off along the stone wall of the building, away from her father's body. Away from the killing ground.

Bolan regained the doorway that he and the others had just left. He hustled swiftly into the hallway that cut through the building. The Executioner hurried on soundless feet.

The merc terrorists over at Jericho's villa had undoubtedly heard the sounds of weapon fire out here in the bleak nowhere.

How would they respond?

As he hurried down the hallway and approached the stairs leading up to the main room, Bolan ran a quick review of what he had seen here so far.

Kennedy has ideas of his own. He's got a market for the cargo he's supposed to be guarding. The buyers are here tonight. The computation lacked one answer: Where is Eve?

Bolan heard raised voices as he approached the stairs to the main room. He paused and listened.

Kennedy was shouting.

"You can't do this, goddammit! We had a deal, you black bastards!"

"Watch your tongue, Mr. Kennedy." A heavily accented African voice; silky but with cold steel in it. "I do not know what is happening outside. But I suggest we leave here at once."

"You're damn right we'll leave here," snarled Kennedy. "And I'm taking my money with me." Then, over his shoulder, he called out: "Hymie—get in here fast!"

Bolan figured Kennedy was calling to the merc who had been guarding Fahima and Bushir. Bolan was about to respond when a door across the hallway burst open and two more African soldiers leveled AK-47s at the Executioner.

Bolan fell to one knee, pumped off two fast rounds from the Galil but not fast enough to stop one of the soldiers firing his own fast round.

But accurate enough to nail both black troopers with head hits that sent them toppling back into the room in a deadfalling tangle.

Bolan mounted the steps two at a time. He entered the inn's main room, Galil searching for targets.

There were four men in the dining room. A bodyguard, in the same uniform as the men outside; two chunky blacks who looked uncomfortable in their Italian suits. And Kennedy.

The gunfire from the corridor had interrupted their confrontation. All four men spun their attention to the doorway Bolan had burst through.

The bodyguard was already pulling up his rifle.

Bolan took the bodyguard first.

The Galil bucked death as Bolan squeezed the trigger. The bodyguard was tagged o-u-t with a rupturing throat hit that tossed him tumbling back to the floor, taking a table and two chairs with him on the way down.

Someone blew out the candle on the table where the principals of the meeting had been sitting. The room was pitched into darkness. There was a scuffling of movement. Mad and fast.

Bolan sidestepped away from where he had stood, went into a deep crouch. He heard a door opening on the other side of the large room.

He fired two rounds at where he determined the sound was. He heard a groan of pain, desperate in the dark.

Bolan dodged again. A handgun opened up from the far corner of the room. He heard the hiss of a bullet slice past him.

Bolan fired to the right of the pistol shot. He darted sideways himself a microsecond after triggering the round. He was not rewarded with the sound of a hit. Bolan's opponent knew how to handle a firefight in the dark, too. Bolan's target was constantly moving. On the offensive.

Two heartbeats. The open doorway was now visible, a deep gray. And empty. Another pistol shot slammed through the darkness. Another tongue of dirty flame across the room.

Bolan heard the darkness as if it were breathing, and divined through a mix of gambling and the intense will of the air itself that his opponent would choose to dodge to the right again. That is where he fired.

He knew he was on the money when a wet rattle bubbled from a body with a sound that no man can fake. The sound of death.

The noisy collapse was succeeded by a hushed stillness in the dining room.

Bolan could hear sounds of assault from outside. Doors were thrown open, running men were entering the inn.

Within seconds the lead invaders were silhouetted in the grayness of the open doorway. Bolan blew away three of them instantly, with three shots and unerring accuracy. His was an inexhaustible command of judgment. The remaining soldiers scampered out of sight for cover, back the way they had come. There were sounds of retreat in the darkness.

Bolan utilized the fleeing seconds before more soldiers came. He moved to where the body of the handgun-wielder had fallen. He looked closely in the gloom.

He was looking into the dead face of one of Kennedy's Italian-togged black customers.

The other buyer was also dead, visibly crumpled near the door. So the first cry in the dark had been that one's last.

And Kennedy was gone.

Bolan moved through the doorway. He was into starlight.

There was troop movement from several areas in and around the small village. The activity centered in the street fronting the inn. Bolan swiftly trotted around to the back of the ancient stone building, then cut off diagonally in a line toward the dunes. His senses were attuned to perceptions of the enemy, and informed him that the deployment numbered ten or twelve men at most, although they were widely scattered and dangerously answerable to no one.

Kennedy could not backtrack through the tunnel to the villa. Bolan recalled meeting those black troopers as he was first helping Fahima and her father to escape. The soldiers had looked like they were on their way to where the girl and her father were hidden. The Africans therefore knew of the room with two doors and Kennedy's "secret" tunnel. Something had gone down here at the inn. Kennedy would know that they knew, because it had just happened.

Kennedy's actions in his office earlier, when Bolan had been watching him, told Bolan that Kennedy was alone on this except for the merc Hymie, no doubt promised a slice of the action. Not even Doyle, Kennedy's second-in-command, knew about what Kennedy had been up to.

Kennedy's probable course of action would be to cut across the open terrain and get back inside the

villa, utilizing his knowledge of security of the Jeri
cho property.

Bolan had to make Kennedy talk.

Kennedy knew where Evita Aguilar was.

But Bolan had to find him first.

11

Kennedy jogged through the night, listening to the sounds of his own labored breathing.

The village of Bishabia, and gunfire, receded to lower ground behind him. He was moving in a zigzag course toward the walls of Leonard Jericho's villa a quarter mile away. He planned a slip back in via his office window. He would bluff his way out of this, whatever happened.

Kennedy's main concern was Mike Rideout. Or whatever the guy's real name was. Kennedy had little doubt that ''Rideout'' would be hot on his trail, and closing fast, at this very moment.

Kennedy paused when the ground suddenly angled downward. The village lights and activity dipped out of sight behind him.

The merc swung around and crouched, listening. He was sure he could hear very light footfalls gaining on him, rapidly approaching from the direction of the village.

Kennedy estimated his pursuer to be about one hundred yards away. Time enough to set a trap.

He unhitched the compact transceiver from his

belt. The radio was Kennedy's contact to Doyle and the other mercs in the villa. Kennedy knew Doyle would be going berserk trying to raise him on the radio the minute they heard the uproar from the village and couldn't find Kennedy. There would be plenty of squawking over the transceiver right now.

Kennedy ran to a nearby ridge in the rock and sand terrain. He placed the transceiver in a shallow surface gully. He flicked a tiny switch, activating the unit. It started crackling.

Kennedy ran back to his previous position. He bellied out prone. He swung the Largo-Star machine gun around by its leather strap into firing posture. Less than fifteen seconds had elapsed since he first paused and listened for the sounds of Rideout's approach.

He would be waiting when the desert starlight silhouetted Rideout's approaching form.

"Boss! What the hell's going on? Do you read me? Are you in the village?" The sounds from the transceiver crackled clearly in the night. *"Come in, goddammit!"*

Enough time had passed, thought Kennedy. Where the hell is he?

"Right behind you." A cool voice answered his thoughts. "Drop your gun. Turn over slowly."

Kennedy swung around onto his back, the Largo-Star blazing.

Mack Bolan had not expected a man like Kennedy to be taken alive. Bolan tried. But the main thing was Bolan staying alive. *He had to find Eve.*

He leaped aside in the instant of time it took Kennedy to twist around.

Kennedy's burst slashed across the space occupied by Rideout's voice. Except that the origin of the voice was moving as fast as a voice could carry across a still desert night, and had slipped out of target acquisition even as the words were sinking in.

Bolan had slid in one process from a voice in the dark to a guy who was out of the picture.

Now Kennedy's execution was fast work. The Galil in Bolan's grip thundered three times in rapid fire. For good measure. Three heavy slugs exploded through living matter, rendering it deceased, spinning Kennedy into a dead man's roll across the ground, leaving a glistening trail of bloodied sand in his wake.

Bolan shoulder-slung his own rifle and picked up the dead man's chopper and an extra ammo clip. Then he hotfooted to the spot where Kennedy's transceiver was still crackling.

Doyle's voice.

"Does anyone read me? Is anyone there?"

Bolan depressed the transmitting button, then started out of there.

"Yeah, yeah," he growled irritably. "Hold on to your shirt!" He was already jogging away from Kennedy's body as he spoke to Doyle. "I'm all right."

He was approximating Kennedy's speech pattern.

He counted on the airwaves and tension of the moment to do the rest. It did.

"Top, what the hell's going on down there?" came Doyle's voice. *"Are you in the village? Do you need backup?"*

"Negative. Get ready to lift off. Ten minutes from now, whether I'm back or not. The pilots have the coordinates?"

"I gave 'em the same ones you gave me. Whadaya mean, if you're not back?"

"I'll catch up," snarled Bolan. "Don't disobey orders. I have something for Mr. Jericho."

Which was true enough, figured Bolan. He arced around, back toward the village at a steady gallop, hoping like hell that ten minutes would be enough time.

Bolan could not make out the type of markings of the truck that had been sent out of the village to investigate his shots. His hearing told him it was a heavy-duty personnel carrier.

The machine was speeding in his direction, bumping across the rough ground.

No headlights.

That confirmed it for Bolan.

The bulky shape of the truck emerged from the gloom, along a route predicted by the Executioner who was crouched off to the side and out of the truck's way. He could discern four men riding in the back of the truck. The vehicle was crashing along at fifty or more miles per.

Bolan opened fire with the newly acquired Largo-Star. He directed his initial stream of fire at the front cab of the racing truck. He could not see clearly into the cab. He didn't need to.

He heard shattering glass.

A scream.

He kept on firing. The lightweight machine gun stuttered in his fists, illuminating the desert night with its muzzle flashes.

The truck veered too sharply. The vehicle seemed to hang suspended in time and space for several moments in a sickening two-wheel tilt.

Shouts from the falling men in the back.

The lurching vehicle lost its battle with gravity. It flipped onto its side. Momentum still pushed the truck through the rock and sand in a grinding forward plow.

Bolan closed in. He discerned a guy's body trapped between the vehicle and hard dirt as the truck skidded along, mashing that particular attacker's torso into hamburger amid a barely human squealing that ended very abruptly.

Bolan moved in on the remaining three hardguys. In the Terrorist Wars, it was shoot or be shot as soon as your cover was blown. That fact John Phoenix knew very well; its implacable message was carved in the flesh of the campaigns already, now, part of his history.

History spoke again as a blistering fire track spat from the Largo-Star into the three-man night, turning it into a howling dark hole of damnation and wet, sticky, glistening desert sand. Bone shards exploded from body sacks in the trajectory of the Largo-Star's death spew—and the night became death for three non-notable terror creeps, a night of darkness as everlasting as would be the kind of war that brings such death. The Terrorist Wars. The War of Evolution. Here, in this damned desert of hellfire and moaning death.

Bolan saw a man's open chest bubble in the starlight. Twenty feet away from him, the soldier had been opened from top to bottom.

He veered away from the killing ground after that. He closed in on the village from a new direction. A stopwatch in his mind kept track of the passing seconds. He gave himself seven more minutes to fix this paramilitary force that had dared penetrate deep into Libya and secrete the sort of cargo about to be airlifted from the Jericho villa.

The African force here might still try to rush the villa and acquire Kennedy's purloined cargo for themselves by force. The only way to avoid such a strategic misfortune would be to deal these troops a decisive blow now, while they were uncertain, before they had time to move right.

Bolan would chew through all of these double-dealers until he found Eve.

He would use the tunnel leading from the inn back to what had been Kennedy's office. There would be no one to guard that route. Not at the inn end, anyway. Those choppers were going to lift off and "Mike Rideout" wanted to be on board. Those aircraft and the cargo would be on their way to Lenny Jericho. And Santos. And Eve.

He reached the back wall of a mud house in the desert on the outskirts of the village. There would be civilian faces at the front windows of the house, facing the activity of the remaining soldiers in the central street and dirt roads. But back here, nothing.

He stayed close to the clay-hard, stonelike building and moved swiftly around its nearest corner. He was heading along one wall of the house for a look into the street. Bolan had let the sounds of the troops guide him. He judged the majority, or possibly all, of the surviving troops to be in a vicinity not far from this house.

When Bolan reached the corner of the hut that gave onto the narrow mud street, he eyeballed the scene at the center of the village where two rutted roads intercepted. His night vision was attuned to the darkness. He was able to make a clean head count of the uniformed men who crowded around an unmarked desert vehicle that matched the truck already destroyed.

Five soldiers stood around the vehicle. The Africans were heatedly debating among themselves in their own tongue.

The Executioner did not hesitate. He stepped clear of the wall. He remained in shadow. "Live free or die," he called out to toll their fate. He triggered a chattering blast from the Largo-Star.

The debate stopped and the soldiers went diving in all directions. Four of them moved under their own power, two dodging behind the truck, one making for the nearest building doorway, the other hitting the ground with rifle blazing in response to Bolan's fire.

The fifth guard did a brief crazy dance as a stream of screaming slugs stitched him from right to left like the heavy metal scythe of Time itself.

Bolan bent his knees into a low, low crouch and moved to the right. He heard bullets whisper near his ear; heard the ricochets of lead whine off the baked mud wall behind him.

Bolan triggered another short burst from the chopper in his hands. Geysers of dirt erupted in a line across the ground from right to left. Then geysers of blood spurted up as the line of bullets skewered the running target's life and set it up to roast in hell.

This was a major engagement.

The other running man was almost making the safety of the nearest building when another stutter of the machine gun checked the run into a sideways kick. Another hit in a festival of death lapping up losers in the flaming game of mankind's survival.

Bolan slapped a fresh clip into the weapon. He advanced toward the truck, remaining all the time in the shadows along the walls of the village huts.

There remained but two troopers in retreat behind

the personnel carrier parked at the intersection. They both leaned out from opposite ends of the truck and fired simultaneous rounds down the length of the street. They had no idea where Bolan was. He continued advancing.

He was some seventy paces from a point where he estimated he would have a clear shot at both men—when a loud report sounded from the opposite side of the intersection.

A Galil, Bolan knew.

He saw the soldier on the far end of the truck tumble out into unprotected view. The soldier did not need protection now. Most of his back was blown out from an exit wound.

The other soldier ducked out to seek new cover in front of the vehicle.

When the merc terrorist was in his sights, the Executioner offered him his worth, a shower of hot lead and a free ticket to hell.

Then the merc, Hohlstrom, emerged from the front door of Fahima's and Bushir's inn. Hohlstrom held his Galil assault rifle at port arms. Bolan saw that the other man appeared every bit as aware of the danger around them as did Bolan himself.

Bolan approached the Swede. The two men were alone in the darkness.

"That's one I owe you, man," said Bolan.

The burly merc gave an easy shrug.

"Forget it. We need to have a few words in private, Colonel."

Bolan felt a spinal shiver.

"You must have me confused with someone else."

"I don't think I do, Colonel Phoenix."

Bolan's fists wrapped tighter around the Galil. He could see that Hohlstrom did not miss the response. Hohlstrom's free hand was on his holstered side arm.

"Explain, guy."

"Steady," said the Swede. "I know who you are and why you're here. And you don't stand a chance in hell of living another thirty minutes."

12

The tableau held for taut seconds between Mack Bolan and Hohlstrom, the Swedish merc. The two men stood there eyeballing each other in the shadows of Bishabia.

The Huey choppers in the nearby villa were scheduled to take off within five minutes. They were Mack Bolan's last chance to reach Eve.

Hohlstrom knew Bolan's true identity. He knew that Bolan was not Rideout, professional merc.

"You're the Israeli agent," said Bolan. "Let's have it one piece at a time while we're moving." The muzzle of his rifle hovered menacingly as they entered the inn. Hohlstrom kept pace as the two men moved quickly toward the storage room where Bolan had found Fahima and Bushir—and the secret tunnel. "How much do you know about me?"

"I know that you are Colonel Phoenix and that you head an operation code named Stony Man," replied Hohlstrom. "You must be here for the same reason as I."

"Tell me the reason."

"You're here to stop Jericho. We can work together."

"I don't think so. You'll have to delay your mission. There's another angle I'm working."

They entered the tunnel, but not before Bolan set down the Largo-Star. It would be real hard explaining that away. He was counting on his and Hohlstrom's arrival to come so close to the lift off that Kennedy's subordinate, Doyle, would have no time for questions or explanations.

Hohlstrom evidently knew the way into the tunnel from his own intel probes.

"My mission is to destroy the shipment in the lead chopper, whatever it is," said Hohlstrom.

"Then it's a suicide mission."

They were jogging now, single file through the tunnel, Bolan leading the way.

"I'm going to blow that copter to hell, one way or another," insisted Hohlstrom. "The cargo is a product of your government's Nuclear Chemical and Biological program. It cannot be allowed to fall into Arab possession. Libya and terrorism sleep together, you know that." The guy's voice grew especially hard. "There must be no more holocausts in this generation. It cannot be allowed to happen."

Bolan tried a new tack. His last one before having to nullify this harmful ally.

"Hohlstrom, listen. The angle I'm working... we've got an agent in the middle of this. But Jericho knows. He has the woman."

"Woman?"

"A lady named Eve Aguilar. She's a good human being, Hohlstrom." Bolan could see the guy turning it over. He pressed on. "I cannot leave her inside to die. I've got air backup behind me. We may be able to pull that cargo out intact or destroy it and stop any deal between Jericho and Shahkhia, and rescue the woman as well. This doesn't have to be a suicide job for you."

A moment's hesitation from the merc.

Time had slipped away altogether. Hohlstrom could not be allowed to stand in Bolan's way.

They had Eve.

Hohlstrom hesitated, finally nodded.

"Okay, Phoenix. If they've got the woman, we'll get her out safely. If the thing breaks wrong. . .then we do it my way."

"You *try* to do it your way," corrected Bolan. "Me, I'll play it as it comes."

They reached the bottom of the stairs leading up to Kennedy's office. Hohlstrom came forward to Bolan's side.

"All right, guy. For now. . .you call it."

"Your people don't have any idea where we're headed?"

"None. That's why I've waited this long. I want to tear their whole thing down."

"Then we'll tear it down together," said the Executioner.

The conversation had taken less than two minutes.

The men moved up the stairway to the sliding panel into what had been Kennedy's office.

As the iciness of ascending combat-readiness flowed through him, Mack Bolan reflected on the allies with whom this mission had brought him into contact.

Fahima and Bushir. Lansdale. And now Hohlstrom.

And maybe Death.

Death was an ally when it kissed the other side.

On this mission, Death had been no ally at all. Thatcher had known of approaching death and sold out to get money for his family. Fahima had lost her father. Death was all around.

Mack Bolan had to find Eve Aguilar before she too was kissed by the Reaper.

He would tear down the walls of Jericho's world, whatever the man was hiding, to spare her from a bloody end.

That was Bolan's Something Big.

Jericho's Something Big was a nuisance factor he would eliminate en route to his supergoal.

The Executioner was on a collision course with a whole bunch of shit that stood in his way, and he would blast open a path for himself every inch of that way.

A path of rescue from distress—a high path, blazed by sacred fires.

13

April Rose was at the main communications console in the mission-control area of Stony Man Farm.

She ignored an urge to look at the time digits on the rectangular clock beside her, as she had promised herself she would when she caught herself glancing at it three times in one minute only a short while ago.

So far... nothing. No action pattern, no holding pattern, nothing since Jack had parted from Bolan at the airstrip outside Tunis.

Grimaldi was now on call aboard a U.S. carrier cruising the Med.

And April Rose was waiting, keeping vigil....

She looked at the clock anyway. 1430 hours.

With the six-hour time difference, that made it 2030 hours Libyan time.

April Rose was the person whose job was to keep the massive, complex mechanism of Stony Man Farm functioning smoothly. She was also a woman who happened to be very much in love with Mack Bolan.

She tried valiantly to keep her worry under wraps, the way most of the men did who worked around her. She tried not to be a woman.

But it didn't work.

She fretted about Mack Bolan every time her man took off on a new mission in this new war against the forces of international horror.

Hal Brognola came into the room. Stony Man Farm's DC liaison did not directly confront April's inquiring look.

Hal sank into a swivel chair by a smaller console. He stared straight ahead without speaking. He held an unlit cigar between his fingers, but both the stogie and April seemed utterly forgotten.

After a minute, she quietly said, "Hal, what is it?"

He looked at her.

"I just spoke with Layton, the major who's handling this out of the Pentagon's NCB office. Internal Affairs pushed for a briefing and called me in."

"Do we know what it is that Jericho has?"

Brognola finally lit his cigar, but slowly, methodically, as if concentrating on the smallest detail of the procedure.

"The bad news that Jericho has is a live virus called Strain-7. It is a pneumonic virus that has been developed to thrive on dry viscera. Its presence in the human body forces the body's water content to places of maximum dehydration from the heat of body friction. This dries out the flesh real nice for Strain-7. For the victim, it's either death from thirst in ten to twelve minutes, or drowning, literally, from the water intake you need to beat the dehydration fever. That takes two or three minutes.

"The worst minutes imaginable. And the stuff can infect entire populations in days or even hours. It would be an appalling end."

"It's ours, this virus, isn't it?" April asked coldly.

"Yes, April. Well, it was. But it isn't anymore. Now it's Jericho's." The stocky man sat stiffly in the swivel chair, turning the seat idly, in fact nervously. "Okay, we admit it, it's government stuff, acquired from a scientist in the NCB group. The army has been storing it mainly as a resource to assist in the development of its antidote by the government. The original scientist who produced the stuff, as a by-product of his NCB work, is dead. Died of dehydration. Took about an hour. . . ."

"Hal, why does our country get involved in a horror like that?"

"Ask the boys in the NCB outfit," grunted the fed. "As chief of security at the base where the virus was being stored, Thatcher was able to divert the junk to Houston under military guard. It was loaded on a private jet—Jericho's jet, we now know—and Jericho's merc security force was standing by to take it over when that jet landed in Libya."

April felt a sense of terror.

"God help the Mideast if that virus falls into Libyan hands," she murmured. "God help us all."

"You can see why Mossad has an interest in this," said Hal. "Jesus Christ, sometimes I wish I only knew enough to be chasing street hoods like in the old days."

April turned back to the communications console.

"I'm going to contact Jack Grimaldi," she said, "and see if there's any possible way to reach Mack with this."

Hal's stogie was in need of a light again, and again he forgot about it. "We have nothing on Eve Aguilar to pass along to him, right?" he said.

"Right," replied April as she activated the sending unit. "The *Traveler* was the last we know for sure that Eve was alive."

Jack Grimaldi stood at the rail along a deserted stretch of flight deck of the aircraft carrier USS *Fearless*. The supercarrier was cruising Mediterranean waters, 130 miles off Libya's Gulf of Sidra, on White House sanctioned maneuvers. The *Fearless* glided as smoothly as a skater on ice. The dark sea, far below Grimaldi, was a choppy panoply of sparkling wet stars and moonlight that mirrored the night sky overhead.

The *Fearless* was a floating city. The warship was home to five thousand sailors and airmen for months at a time. The five-deck seagoing airport was a warren of passages, offices, shops, mess halls and crew quarters; a numbering system had been devised to keep people from getting lost. Someone had mentioned to Grimaldi that the Eiffel Tower, if laid on its side, would overhang the flight deck by only five feet.

The Stony Man flyboy was smoking a cigarette, trying to relax.

The angled black flight deck was quiet at this hour. The big flattop's two-hundred-thousand horsepower engines, turning her four shafts with their seventy-thousand-pound propellers, could not be heard up here. The incessant roaring, banging and hissing of steam catapult launches and the thumping and snapping of cable-arrested landings, which had been going on since Grimaldi's airlift to the ship from Tunis via a Sikorsky 70L shipboard helicopter, had only minutes ago been called to a halt until more exercises tomorrow morning.

Grimaldi experienced a momentary sense of oneness with the Med, the alluring but historically much fought-over sea.

He could not relax.

That moon overhead, that same panoply of stars, shone down on Mack Bolan at this moment, wherever he was.

If he was still alive.

No way could Grimaldi relax, knowing what he did.

Grimaldi was joined at the rail by an admiral named Fieldhouse. The task force commander was the only man onboard the *Fearless* who knew what Grimaldi knew.

"They told me in Communications that you had to speak with me, Mr. Grimaldi."

Jack did not take his eyes away from the panorama of Mediterranean night.

"What are my chances of violating Libyan airspace without detection? I've got to reach him."

Fieldhouse paused to frame a reply, balancing the odds in his mind. He nodded at the moonwashed expanse of sea.

"The Gulf of Sidra is where two of our planes made hot contact with two of Libya's Su-22s a while back. Soviet-built fighter planes. Those Sus are at the bottom of that gulf right now. Our intel is that Khaddafi's training program hasn't kept up with the technology he's been acquiring. Yes, his army and airforce do have the equipment to spot you coming in. But whether they actually spot you, and how quickly they respond...well, I'd say you stand a chance of getting in and out again if you fly low. Not a good chance, but some chance. What do you need?"

Grimaldi tossed his cigarette butt over the rail.

He had needed some few minutes alone after receiving the communiqué from Stony Man Farm. He came up here from the ship's communications room, had filled his lungs with gulps of ocean air and half a cigarette. It was enough.

He could handle it.

"What have you got that will get me in fast under their radar grid and punch hard when I get there, Admiral?"

"My recommendation would be our new Boeing 1041 multirole V/STOL," said Fieldhouse. "We have two of them below, on twenty-four standby—one of them without markings."

"What kind of armament?"

"The 1041 has air-to-air and air-to-surface missile capability. Unfortunately it's not equipped with cannon or machine guns. But with a flight speed of about Mach 0.8, I'd say she's your best bet for the kind of hit you seem to have in mind." The navy man studied the Stony Man pilot with a long look. "This is a very bizarre mission, Mr. Grimaldi."

Grimaldi grunted grim acknowledgment. "It's a bizarre world, Admiral. I'll take your advice. The 1041 it is. Lead the way, please."

Fieldhouse moved down to the principal hangar belowdecks.

Grimaldi tossed one last look over his shoulder at the dark beauty of the Med. He wondered if the sea would still sparkle in the moonlight and reflect those stars the way it did right now—after everyone was dead.

Yeah. Everyone.

Strain-7— No one knew for sure exactly what it was capable of. The worst possible guess, of course, was that it had the capability of killing off every human being on the face of the earth. . . .

It was very literally a matter of life and death for most of the planet that Mack Bolan now held in his hands.

And Mack did not know it.

Ah, friend, soldier, go carefully in this night. This dark night in your endless war.

Jack Grimaldi knew that his best friend was walking a lonely trail now, and that he was risking all because he did not want to further endanger Eve Aguilar's life; and yes, Grimaldi could identify with that. The pilot was a man of well-defined, fiery Italian temperament who appreciated completely the powers of love and caring that were the lifeblood of his race and the driving force of a bigger-than-life dude named Mack Bolan. The guy would've made a damn good *Italiano*.

Grimaldi and Fieldhouse entered the cavernous hangar of the *Fearless*. Planes, men, activity, the smell of grease and oil were everywhere. Noise echoed off the towering steel walls.

Fieldhouse angled off to make arrangements for Grimaldi's briefing and takeoff.

Grimaldi walked over to the plane he would be flying into Libya. He checked out the aircraft with a growing sense of approval.

The two-passenger V/STOL boasted a forty-one-foot wingspan, and a fuselage length of about forty-eight feet. The aircraft was shiny and new, without markings, and Grimaldi hoped he could bring her back in the same condition. The Boeing 1041 was excellent. It would do, hell yeah.

Jack Grimaldi was finished sitting on his tail.

14

Bolan and Hohlstrom moved toward Doyle who awaited them by one of the gunships. Four of Kennedy's mercs were already aboard the second gunship. Three men had climbed aboard the copter that carried the cargo. Bruner and Teckert were aboard the aircraft that Doyle stood next to. The ground throbbed and the air thundered with the powerful whistling of revving turbines.

As Rideout and Hohlstrom approached, Doyle called out to them loud enough to be heard above the waves of sound.

"Where the hell have you guys been? Queer for each other or somethin'?" With a wave of his arm, the guy gave out the orders. "Get in the fuckin' chopper. You guys are riding with Teckert and Bruner. Move it!"

Doyle turned and jumped aboard the mother ship. He slammed shut the side hatchdoor. Seconds later, the aircraft shuddered and lifted off. It was immediately followed by gunship number two.

Bolan and Hohlstrom climbed into the chopper where Bruner and Teckert were waiting. Bolan closed the side door. The pilot raised his collective pitch control lever and the third big bird lifted off.

Bolan could see the floodlit grounds of the villa recede beneath them. The Huey cleared the walls, then heeled over and slid gently away into the Sahara night, traveling in what Bolan determined to be a southerly direction.

Like the other men, Bolan had grabbed a wallstrap for support. He glanced at Bruner and Teckert, then at Hohlstrom, but the constant high-pitched whine from the copter's transmission directly overhead made any conversation difficult.

The pilot reached the desired altitude, about three thousand feet. The climb leveled off into a smooth forward cruise.

Bolan gazed beyond the Huey's Plexiglas windows and saw that the three choppers were maintaining a loose formation, twelve to fifteen rotor widths apart, with the two gunships slightly higher to either side of the copter that transported Doyle and the cargo.

Bolan's Galil was strapped over his left shoulder. His belt was equipped with grenades. His right hand never drifted far from the Browning hi-power riding low at his right hip.

Each of the other men toted equal fire power. Teckert and Bruner both carried .357 Magnums on the hip in fast-draw holster. Teckert was gripping a Beretta Model 70 assault rifle in his right hand while the German wore his Galil by the shoulder strap, like Bolan. Hohlstrom had his Beretta pistol in a shoulder holster. An AK-47 was strapped across his left shoulder.

Bolan admired the way Hohlstrom carried himself. The guy was a pro. Mack Bolan preferred working solo or with the trusted members of his Stony Man operation in backup. But since he and the "Swede" were in a situation where they had to work side by side, he was glad this unexpected partner was a man by all appearances exceedingly capable and tough.

As the men grouped together in the bay of the aircraft, Teckert looked at Hohlstrom with the attitude of someone about to shout above the constant, near deafening engine roar from over their head. But he did not speak.

Teckert *moved*.

So did Mack Bolan.

Bolan saw it coming. He dropped to his left, unleathered the Browning, and stayed put.

Hohlstrom had leaned forward to give an ear to Teckert, expecting the guy to shout something as Teckert had appeared ready to do. But yeah, Hohlstrom saw it coming too. He jerked back, tugging his Beretta from its underarm holster in a lightning-fast cross draw. Exceedingly capable.

Except that it was two-to-one.

Bruner executed a fast downward judo chop with his right hand. The Beretta clattered to the deck from Hohlstrom's fist.

It was a fractured splinter of time. The steady throb from the chopper's machinery grumbled around the scene of violence.

Hohlstrom back-stepped in an attempt to unshoulder the AK-47.

Teckert closed in before Hohlstrom's action was complete. Teckert used both hands to heft the Beretta Model 70 he was toting in his right hand. He smashed the assault rifle, butt forward, full force into Hohlstrom's high forehead. The dull *thwack* carried even above the Huey's engine noise.

Hohlstrom's knees buckled. He slumped to the chopper's deck, at the other men's feet, blood streaming down his face and into his eyes.

Teckert stepped away, the butt of his rifle smeared with red.

Bruner, hoisting up Hohlstrom's Beretta, had swung around to cover Bolan. The German froze, staring into the bore of Bolan's Browning automatic.

It was a standoff.

Bolan shifted the Browning's aim between Bruner and Teckert. Bruner did not drop the Beretta. Teckert had reversed his rifle to take aim on Hohlstrom. Everyone had a gun except the fallen man.

The Israeli agent was stretched out facedown, holding his forehead but not making a sound. The guy was holding his pain inside. He appeared only semiconscious.

Bruner did not blink an eye at the handgun in Bolan's fist. "PUT THAT GUN AWAY, MY FRIEND," he yelled above the engine noise. "THESE ARE DOYLE'S ORDERS!"

Bolan gave a curt nod toward Hohlstrom. He did not holster the Browning. "I WANT TO KNOW ABOUT THIS!"

"HOHLSTROM'S A GODDAMN SPY!" Teckert shouted at Bolan. "AN ISRAELI!"

Bolan retained his two-hand grip in a bent-knee stance, the Browning hi-power continuing to arc between the two standing mercs. *Teckert and Bruner did not know how close they were....*

But a squeeze of Teckert's trigger finger and Hohlstrom would be dead.

Bolan was sizing his options.

"HOHLSTROM'S A BUDDY!" Bolan shouted at the other two. "WHAT PROOF DO YOU HAVE?"

"KENNEDY'S GOT PROOF!" yelled Teckert.

At their feet, Hohlstrom was wiping the blood from his eyes.

Bolan moved around an iota to keep tabs on the chopper pilot up front. The pilot did not turn from his flight controls. The big Huey continued rumbling through the desert night.

Bolan could almost smell the dramatic fuse burning inside this helicopter, getting ready to ignite an explosion.

Bruner stepped wide around Hohlstrom's fallen form, drawn up into a fetal ball a few feet inside the copter's side door.

Bruner unlatched the door and yanked it open.

Freezing desert night air whistled in through the gaping hatchway. The Huey's engine roar and the sounds of the whirling rotor blades overhead pounded in.

"NOW WE FIND OUT ABOUT YOU, MR. RIDEOUT," screamed Bruner.

Teckert, standing next to Bruner, indicated the sprawling figure at their feet with the Beretta assault rifle that he still aimed at Hohlstrom's head. "DOYLE SAYS, YOU ICE THE KIKE!"

The German at Teckert's side was still aiming his Beretta pistol at Bolan's head, and he gave a nod at the desert night speeding by outside the open hatch.

"PUSH HOHLSTROM OUT," Bruner ordered Bolan. "RIGHT NOW."

15

Bolan had only one option.

His advantage was that the two mercs obviously expected "Rideout" to pass this loyalty test. They had no suspicions otherwise. These men just wanted someone else to do their dirty work in disposing of the spy, Hohlstrom.

Only one option: *kill!*

Bolan twisted with a fluid sideways movement, moving suddenly low and to the left of the 9mm Beretta that Bruner was aiming in his direction.

Meanwhile from his position at everyone's feet, Hohlstrom went unnoticed by Bruner and Teckert as both men swung their attention to Bolan's maneuver. They did not see Hohlstrom swiftly ease around the AK-47 that had dropped to the deck beside him.

From a low crouch, to the side of the action, the Executioner squeezed off a well-placed round from the Browning. The automatic barked from Bolan's right fist, stabbing out an orange red pencil of fire.

At the same instant Bruner pulled off a round from his Beretta. He fired at where Bolan had been one eye-blink before.

Bolan did not fire on Bruner. He first needed to

take out Teckert, who stood closest to Hohlstrom and posed the most immediate threat to the fallen Mossad agent.

Bolan's 9mm round frothed apart most of merc Teckert's skull out the chopper's door into the Sahara night racing by directly behind him, followed by what remained of his corpse.

In the same flick of time, Hohlstrom had rolled onto his side and brought the AK tracking upward toward Bruner. A deadly chatter from Hohlstrom's grip spit a burst of shredders that lifted Bruner to the bulkhead of the helicopter and held him there for a moment, his torso bursting apart. Bruner slumped down to the deck. The bulkhead behind where his body had been pinned was riddled, marred with flesh and blood and smoking shreds of clothing.

Hohlstrom pushed himself to his knees, then wiped away the blood that still oozed down into his eyes from his forehead wound. The Mossad man was injured, but holding on. Staying hard.

Bolan swung his focus to the pilot of the chopper.

The pilot was responding to the action. He had punched into the tac net and was shouting into a hand-held mike something that Bolan could not hear. Now the merc pilot was swinging around in his cockpit, tracking toward Bolan with an old-fashioned army issue Colt .45.

Bolan's Browning again penciled death. The pilot pitched over, his near-lifeless body palpitating to final departure on the floor.

Bolan leaped forward and seated himself in the

cockpit. He took control of the Huey, glancing out the Plexiglas for a reading of position on the other two choppers.

Quivers of a past life echoed in from his subconscious: soldiering in the hellgrounds of Vietnam those many years ago, learning all he could about everything involved with surviving in a hostile jungle combat zone; observing things like how to pilot the Hueys, those ever-present big birds of Nam.

The Huey with Doyle was pulling away south and there was nothing Bolan could do to halt it.

The other gunship was responding to the dead pilot's radioed SOS.

The heavily armed chopper was banking around for a kill shot. Bolan reacted quickly, pulling the cyclic control stick hard to his left.

"Hang on!" he shouted over his shoulder at Hohlstrom.

As he spoke, their aircraft was already lurching and dipping in an evasive maneuver.

The other Huey opened fire. Its turret-mounted miniguns rattled off a twin streak of 5.56mm armor-piercing rounds.

A direct raking of the fuselage of Bolan's copter was avoided by his fast evasive response. But the other gunship scored a hit.

Bolan felt the cyclic control stick vibrate wildly in his fist. That was the first warning.

Abrupt silence replaced the screaming whine of the Huey's transmission above and behind Bolan. All engine gauges on the flight-control instrument panel plummeted to zero.

Bolan's chopper had sustained an engine hit. The engine was dead. Bolan had only seconds to react.

To his left side in the cockpit was a collective pitch-control lever that controlled the pitch of the rotors. He rammed it down. With the pitch of the blades flattened, even the whistling outside died away.

Bolan was aiming for autorotation of the blades from the copter's downward momentum.

It was an old trick that worked...sometimes.

It was the only trick he had right now.

The silent Huey went into a descending glide, the air from its downward speed rushing up through the blades, keeping them spinning.

The other gunship opened fire with its machine guns, sending a twin stream of tracer bullets that arced only inches from the Plexiglas near Bolan.

All of Bolan's attention centered on the flight controls and life-or-death gauge readings of the aircraft he was attempting to land.

His Huey was sailing in at a fast, steady, dangerous descent.

He glanced at the tachometer. As the speed of his chopper's drop increased, the autorotation of the blades registered as climbing rpm. The needle edged back into the safe zone.

Bolan's copter angled downward at about seventy knots. The trickiest part was yet to come.

Bolan closely monitored those rpm. The collective

pitch-control lever to his left and the cyclic-control stick to his right both gouged deep furrows into Bolan's palms.

The mother ship of the mission, carrying Kennedy's official number two, Doyle, plus the cargo and the knowledge of Eva Aguilar's whereabouts, was long gone. Gunship number two was probably aiming to land on the desert floor close below, waiting for Bolan and Hohlstrom to crash—and waiting to kill them if they survived.

Bolan flicked on his landing lights, illuminating the first traces of rocky sand dunes beneath him. Once Bolan had fixed his position, he punched off the lights.

At some fifty feet from the ground, still descending with gut-wrenching speed, Mack Bolan ripped back on the cyclic lever.

The Huey nosed sharply upward until the helicopter almost stood on its tail. The rate of dive was arrested as if a tug wire had been yanked, bringing Bolan's tipped machine to a momentary midair stop.

This was the critical point of a dead-engine landing.

Truth time.

At the precise moment that the Huey had airbraked with its nose at a new upward forty-five degree angle, the warrior in the cockpit shoved the cyclic forward again.

The chopper's rounded nose dropped into a level position. Bolan was fiercely aware of the blood pounding in his ears from the pitching rate of descent followed by the sudden halt.

The Huey was now only fifteen, twenty feet above the desert floor. Hanging there. The rotors still going.

Bolan eased in on the collective once more, very gently.

The ground came up toward the ship like a hurtling wall. The helicopter hit zero with a crunch, a stunning stop made mad by all the framework and the components and the carried objects continuing on down as if headed for the center of the earth.

It was a stubbornness of physics that led to a grinding, screeching crash as a full load of metal-toting gravity collided with the surface of that earth.

Carried objects included Bolan and Hohlstrom, who were pounded into their crash positions as if by a giant fist. Bolan was winded, his perceptions temporarily shattered, his side bruised by the controls as the wrecked helicopter tilted forward brutally, suddenly burying its undernose in a sand dune.

The smell of gasoline filled the cockpit. Actual vapor stung Bolan's nose.

"Out of here! Out, out!" he called, as if automatically overcoming shock and pain with roaring movement.

Hohlstrom was lifting himself once more from the helicopter's floor. The impact of the landing had knocked him down and damn near out again, then the nose-tilt had sent him sprawling.

Like a man skilled at being big, he had moved through the ordeal with a relaxed rolling motion that had spared him major hurt or rupture. Any puncturing was reserved for the gas line.

Now Hohlstrom was up and leaping from the gas-reeking wreck. But Bolan had already moved clear, was indeed returning for Hohlstrom, his mouth forming further commands to get the hell out.

The vapor seemed to sizzle before it suddenly burst into a mighty *whump*, blasting a fireball of broiling red and orange out across the crash site, spreading a wave of scorching acrid hell that gobbled at the back of the Mossad agent.

Hohlstrom nose-dived toward Bolan, the heat mushrooming over him. He was safe—and his face was half-buried in gritty sand.

Mack Bolan, his features ablaze from the glow that illuminated the environment like sunrise in a gray dawn sky, reached Hohlstrom and hauled him to his feet.

"Here comes whatever's next," he said, glancing up. The two men were near a ridge that would hide them from what was soon to be a landing zone. And a kill zone.

Gunship number two now touched down there. The pilot brought his engine to ground idle. The only sound in the night was a lazy, sibilant *swoosh* as the rotors of the healthy Huey continued to turn. Its lights came on, revealing the barren Sahara topography around it.

Behind Bolan, the injured Mossad agent stood steady. He slammed a fresh clip into his AK-47.

"Get *down!*" growled Bolan.

He had discerned movement around the open hatch of the other Huey.

A volley of automatic weapons fire suddenly rattled in the desert quiet. Projectiles whistled by inches above the sprawled figures of Bolan and Hohlstrom, buzzing like a cloud of angry hornets.

Hohlstrom's face was inches from Bolan's on the sand. The Mossad man's eyes were hard and steady.

"We're pinned good," he said.

"Only on our right flank," responded Bolan. "I saw a ridge to our left before I cut the landing lights. Let's make it there before those men swing around behind us."

"I'm with you!" growled Hohlstrom. "Lead the way."

Bolan did exactly that.

The gunfire from the other chopper ceased. Obviously the gunship commander was trying to decide how to play this.

Bolan and Hohlstrom hustled in a low jog toward the sand dune that Bolan had indicated. Both men carried their weapons, ready to use them on anything that moved in the shadows cast in weird, multicolored hues from the other copter's landing lights.

Nothing physical came at them; only the magnified voice of the pilot from the other gunship.

"ARE YOU ALIVE OVER THERE?"

The demand was firm and authoritative.

Bolan's impression of the surrounding terrain, briefly glimpsed as he had brought down the chopper, proved accurate.

The ridge of sand dune that he and Hohlstrom now held visibly, extended to their left in a lazy sweep around and slightly above the open ground separating the two copters. It embraced the rear flank of the pilot's position.

Bolan considered whether the pilot was aware of this.

Whether he was baiting a trap.

Hohlstrom spoke in a whisper, reading Bolan's mind.

"Okay, it just might work. I'm with you, Phoenix. Let's take those bums *out.*"

The two fighting men were already moving at a low trot, beneath cover of the stony ridge.

They had not gone five yards before more weapons fire erupted from the vicinity of the second gunship. The rocky ground seemed to pound beneath Bolan's feet as orange silver strobelike flashes wildly illuminated the wilderness.

Mack Bolan and Hohlstrom continued along their course beneath cover of the ridge, swinging around to the other force's side flank.

Death was in the air.

Executioner at work!

16

The gunship pilot could feel it, could sense it, the death in the air. Something had gone wrong. The orders were for tight formation in forward flight, not garbled messages over the radio and a precipitate drop to the ground under fire.

He glanced at the four other mercs under his command. They stood beside him in the open side door of their gunship.

"You men fall out here and flank out toward our nose," he ordered. He looked at the armed navigator, unable even to remember the guy's name. "You come with me. We'll flank out toward the left. Keep your heads down. All right, let's go. Kill anything that moves."

The five men went EVA and started moving in the darkness toward the other helicopter.

He noticed for the first time that a ridge ran north-south to their right flank. It was possible that . . . .

The night spat chattering gunfire from atop the ridge.

Two mercs emitted short grunts as they were spun around by the impact of the bullets, flurries of twisted arms and legs sprawling to the desert floor.

"Mother of God!" gasped the pilot in a scramble back toward cover.

The machine gun on the ridge stuttered again.

He and the navigator were already making a hurried dash back to the chopper when the pilot heard bullets snuff out the life behind him; he heard the sound of the dead man toppling to the sand.

As fast as he was pumping his legs, as close as his Huey gunship was, time stood still for the merc during that short dash for safety. His heart was hammering. He had the disjointed realization that his forehead wore a glaze of sweat despite the chilled night air.

There was no more gunfire.

Now what the hell?

He sensed movement from his right, from around the tail of the Huey gunship.

From his left, the other remaining merc shouted something unintelligible. More gunfire from that side.

But the pilot only had eyes on the big figure, gripping a Galil in his hands, who stepped into the red-splashed illumination of the copter's landing lights.

The big dude was moving toward him. The rosy glow of the Huey's lights were reflected, even from this distance, by the man's eyes that looked like chips of ice.

He brought up his AK-47 on the imposing combat figure striding toward him, knowing, even as his life

survival instincts flared into crystal clarity, that he
was too late.

The sharp report of the Galil was the last sound he
ever heard.

Bolan heard the exchange of fire between Hohlstrom
and the remaining merc, toward the front of the gunship.

Then the gunfire stopped. The Sahara night was
utterly silent except for the ghostly whooshing of the
gunship's rotor blades rotating in idle.

There was no sign of Hohlstrom.

Bolan moved across the field of dead men, jogging
cautiously up to the rocky ridge where Hohlstrom
had been inflicting his hits.

Bolan felt a sick premonition that was affirmed the
moment he topped the ridge.

The "Swede" was prone in a cleft in the rocks,
which had given him a clear view of the ground surrounding the second gunship.

The Mossad agent was not moving.

Bolan bit off a curse as he approached the motion-
less form. He knelt beside his partner in this firefight
and turned the man onto his side.

Hohlstrom had stopped at least one bullet before
taking out the remaining merc down below. The
agent's throat was a pulpy raw mess. This fighter
would fight no more. He and the merc may have died
at the same time; certainly within seconds of each
other.

Bolan stood. He paused there in the cool night, above the body of his fallen ally. Mack Bolan listened. He watched.

Nothing moved.

He shared this desolation with the dead.

But his mind was also on the second gunship, which was operational. It was a slim chance, but he might still be able to trace Doyle to the south, in the mother ship with that mysterious cargo that all of the mercenaries here had died to protect.

Bolan slipped a silent salute to a good man who had sacrificed his life for a good cause. Then the Executioner turned from Hohlstrom's fallen form and started back down the ridge of that sand dune toward the idling helicopter.

When the sky came alive.

A whistling whine was piercing the darkness to the north. Two jets lanced in with their underbelly floodlamps casting quarter-mile pools of light in front of them on the desert floor as they screamed toward him.

When they were about a quarter mile away, the plane to Bolan's right veered sharply off from its mate, in an easterly sweep. Must be that the pilot of the second gunship had radioed ahead that they were going down, but had not had time for the exact coordinates. The jets were searching. From his Stony Man briefings, Bolan figured that the aircraft left for him to contend with was a Soviet-made Su-22.

Bolan hoped he could make it to the protection of

the idling gunship before the Su-22 coming his way could spot him. His numbers had tumbled away, however. Another couple of heartbeats and that big warplane would be directly overhead, and Bolan was less than halfway down the sandy ridge that receded toward the Huey. He would be pinned beneath the harsh glare of the big jet's lights. The Libyan pilot was dusting the rolling terrain at a snug eight hundred feet. He would not miss Bolan.

Bolan acted.

He thumbed the Galil onto its grenade launcher mode. He unclipped one of the grenades belted to his hip. He fed the grenade into the weapon's launcher apparatus.

The Galil is supposed to be fired from the tripod position when utilizing the grenade launcher. Bolan did not have time for that. He braced himself for the coming recoil. He triggered the assault rifle. Time had run out.

The Galil's recoil practically knocked Mack Bolan backward off his feet. The world screeched of madness from the big Su-22's engines. Armageddon would sound like this.

The HE impacted the Su-22 seconds after it passed over Bolan's head. The Soviet-supplied warplane blossomed into a wildfire flower. The jet disappeared for an instant, swallowed up by explosion. Then the scorched skeletal remains of the aircraft were visible hurtling into the gloom.

Scratch one Su-22.

Bolan scanned the night. Then he continued jogging toward the Huey gunship, still idling eighty yards away. He quickly spotted the other Libyan jet, maybe two miles to the east.

The second jet was responding by heeling around for a run of its own at Bolan.

It was happening in no time at all.

The Libyan jet sailed in with its wing-mounted miniguns blasting wide open.

17

The warplane, still a mile away in the night sky but gaining fast, fired off an air-to-surface missile that fingered out on a smoking trajectory toward the grounded Huey.

Bolan saw it coming, dived, flattened himself to the sand beneath him as the Atoll missile hit and blew the Huey apart with a ground-shivering blast. The heat of the deafening blast pushed down on Bolan's back.

Bolan got to his feet as soon as the fireball rippled the airwaves above him. He swung around to meet the Su-22 that was almost overhead, its machine guns resuming heavy fire. Spurts of rock and sand geysered up in approaching lines, gaining on his position. He was slapping another grenade onto the ARM's launcher attachment when sounds of another approaching jet aircraft split the night.

The Libyan pilot wheeled away, abruptly changing flight course.

The new arrival streaked by low overhead with a slight salutary tip of the wings at the man on the ground.

Bolan saw that this was not another jet with Libyan markings. This was a Short Take-Off and Landing craft. Who else but?

Jack Grimaldi.

For a few moments, both aircraft were swallowed up by the night sky to the west.

Then Grimaldi's contact with the enemy got hot.

The 1041 fired a missile. Bolan tracked the red flame of its tail, then saw another hellfire eruption of flash and flame that lit up the sky overhead like summer lightning. The sound soon followed.

The night was still reverberating when the V/STOL returned. The unmarked American fighter jet hovered overhead for a few seconds. Then the pilot set her down twenty yards away from where Bolan stood.

The hatch popped open. A familiar figure appeared, tugging off his flight helmet.

Grimaldi, yeah.

The pilot from Stony Man dropped to the ground from the aircraft's wing. The two men approached each other. Grimaldi was all smiles.

Bolan raised his voice to be heard above the noise of the idling V/STOL.

"Welcome to Libya, Jack! Another one I owe you."

Grimaldi seemed not to hear the thanks. He gazed at the scene of carnage around them: the two demolished Hueys and the men who had died. Then he scanned the northern sky.

"I suggest that we haul ass before any more of those Su-22s decide to play backup."

They hoofed back to the V/STOL and got onto the wing.

"Those Libyan planes were sent by Shahkhia," said Bolan as they climbed into the two-man plane and donned their helmets, communicating through the jet's radio setup. "I think we've seen everything he can afford to send—and lose. But get us out of here, Jack. Any word from Hal's intel on where Jericho is supposed to meet with Colonel Shahkhia?"

Grimaldi slammed shut the Plexiglas bubble above their heads.

"Afraid not. Nothing on Eve, either. I'm sorry, Mack."

"She'll be wherever Jericho and Santos are," said Bolan. "Wherever these choppers were originally heading."

It was then that Jack Grimaldi delivered his verbal bombshell. In a few succinct words above the engine roar of the aircraft, the pilot briefed the Executioner on exactly what it was that General Arnold Thatcher had channeled to Leonard Jericho. The facts regarding Strain-7. Just the facts.

Bolan absorbed it in silence. There was plenty to absorb.

With a sudden, mighty thrust, the V/STOL picked itself up off the Sahara sands and kicked forward with body-jarring speed.

The scene of carnage beyond the cockpit blurred into memory. The Boeing 1041 became gone from that place.

"This darling's equipped with computer capability," said Grimaldi through the headset linkup. "I'm playing with coordinates over a satellite map right now. There's Aujila oasis forty miles south of here. That's *all* there is."

"Could be it," muttered Bolan. He tried to remain wary of the budding hope he felt at the news.

"There's a small military installation at Aujila," the pilot relayed from his computer map. "It's an outpost for desert patrol. No other settlements of any sort for a couple of hundred miles. And this is current satellite observation."

"Then Aujila it is," said Bolan. "How far?"

The V/STOL was skimming the desert at several hundred feet. Grimaldi was proving once again that he was an ace in the cockpit.

"Buddy, we are. . . here. Those are the lights of the oasis up to your left."

The cluster of light was now clearly visible in the clean desert air from an estimated distance of two miles. The lights were the only thing visible in the darkness.

Grimaldi did not angle the V/STOL in that direction. He held their distance by subtle control of the tilt-jet ability to brake, slip, drop.

"A recon pass is out," said Bolan. "But this is the end of the trail, Jack. That's where they've got Eve.

That's where this whole deal is going to go down. How close can you land me without drawing ear or eye to us?"

Another short pause as the aircraft's computer up front fed more data to Grimaldi.

"This is a primary air lane between Benghazi and most of South Africa," reported the pilot as he hovered the plane. "If they did hear anything from the base, they might not think too much of someone zipping along a tad low. I could touch down unnoticed, oh, say, one and a half miles away from there. How would that do?"

"That would do beautifully. Then I want you to hold back with the air support. But watch for me. I'll have Eve with me."

"Down we go," said Grimaldi.

The V/STOL aircraft's jet sounds became muted as the pilot patterned into a landing descent.

Grimaldi had set them down without detection. The inky stillness surrounded them in chill silence.

Bolan went EVA. He made the short drop to the ground from the aircraft's wing, carrying a canvas bag of supplies thoughtfully provided by Grimaldi and left near his seat in the cockpit.

"How long do I wait before I worry?" Grimaldi called down to Bolan.

The Executioner eyed the luminous hands of his watch. He calculated quick mental computations regarding time, distance and what he must accomplish.

"Give me forty minutes, Jack." He was applying

black facial camouflage ointment while he spoke. "Come in from this direction. I'll build my play around that." He repacked the tube of ointment and returned it to the satchel. Then he withdrew from the satchel's depths the heavy metal of his familiar armaments, including Starlite scope. "Thanks, Jack. Thanks for everything."

"Mack, wait! Give me word on what to expect. What's your strategy?"

Bolan paused and looked back at the pilot. Time was running out, but Grimaldi's concern was real.

"This one is on the heartbeat, buddy. I've got to find Eve and I've got to put this thing of Jericho's out of business." He thought briefly of Hohlstrom, and of the supreme sacrifice the Mossad agent had made. "For the living, and for the dead. You just give me that forty minutes. If I'm not out by then, I won't be coming out."

Grimaldi grunted. "I'll be there," he promised.

Mack Bolan gave the pilot a raised fist salute that Grimaldi returned.

The Executioner turned and put that place behind him, moving at a fast trot into the night.

Toward Eve.

Toward a confrontation with his own fate.

18

The figure in torn, cordite-smelling camou fatigues sprinted across the undulating desert terrain. He was one with the night around him. The added weight of weapons and armament strapped across his body did not slow him.

The big .44 AutoMag mini-howitzer and the 9mm Beretta Belle were back where they belonged, leathered on his right hip and in a quick-draw underarm shoulder holster respectively. Bolan was outfitted much as he had been less than two days ago when this mission had begun for him in the waters of Exuma Cay in the Bahamas. Explosives courtesy of both Kennedy and Grimaldi rode securely on his left hip. Knives, garrotes and other instruments of silent death were secured at various points.

Vague, indeterminate sounds, a sense of activity, carried to him across the wide open spaces from the vicinity of the base, more than a mile away, as he made his approach.

Except for this impression of activity, there was silence. Cold shadows hugged the lunarlike landscape. There was no sign of life out here beyond the Aujila oasis and the base situated there.

There was only Bolan.

Alone with his thoughts.

Mack Bolan preferred a combat posture as the quiet infiltrator. Bolan the penetration specialist was in his natural element.

He covered the distance without incident.

Bolan's breathing was steady as he jogged that hilly distance. He was pacing himself for the firefight that lay ahead. His strength would be far from sapped at the end of this run.

He did not try to block his thoughts from touching on the woman he hoped to locate and rescue in that military compound.

In most ways Eve Aguilar was what this mission was all about, symbolically as well as literally.

Thinking about it pushed him on, harder and faster.

He thought about a rustic bungalow on Douglas Lake in the Smoky Mountains of eastern Tennessee, some two hundred miles from Nashville.

That was the last time Mack Bolan had been with Big Eve. He remembered it now with vivid, aching clarity.

At the time, Bolan had just completed shaking up the Nashville operation of Nick Copa as part of the Executioner's war against the Mafia.

At the windup of that Music City action, Hal Brognola had approached Bolan with an incredible offer: Presidential pardon, full amnesty for past illegalities, a new identity and a chair on the National Security Council. . . *if* Mack Bolan would redirect his capabilities toward a newly defined cause.

Bolan and Evita Aguilar had already made arrangements for a rendezvous back then, a plan for some R & R together at the close of Bolan's Tennessee Smash, since both he and Eve were between missions.

The secluded cabin, which had been theirs for a day and a night, had commanded a view of a breathtaking pine valley. This was Davy Crockett country. Old Andy Jackson, too. Hero country, yeah. The backbone of the American spirit, set amid some of the most spectacular natural beauty east of the Mississippi.

For much too short a time, it had seemed as if that paradise had belonged to two soldiers named Mack Bolan and Eve Aguilar.

They had pleasured themselves with each other sexually, sure, and with each other's intellect. But every bit as important was the sense of shared space that they had experienced, even while allowing each other their separate, personal thoughts during their brief time together.

Eve obviously had things on her mind as much as Bolan did. They had planned on spending more than a scant twenty-four hours together. But now Brognola was waiting for Bolan's response, and the plans had to be alerted.

During those twenty-four hours in their Smoky

Mountain paradise, Bolan and Eve had separated for some five hours.

Bolan hiked to a secluded cove for some solitary roaming and thinking. When he returned to their cabin near dusk, he had found Eve sitting on a rock formation overlooking the lake.

She was dressed in light blue sweater and slacks, her midnight-black hair ruffled by the pine-scented breeze. She looked stunning.

I walked up to her and though I could tell she heard me approach, she did not turn from gazing out over the expanse of water that was silver with the reflection of the setting sun.

"It's beautiful," I said.

She nodded gently.

"Si. Very beautiful."

At the last word, a tear leaked from the lady's eye and fell down her cheek.

I sat on the rock beside her. She leaned into me and my arm went around her. To this day I can still feel the natural warmth of her.

I told her, quietly and gently, "Sometimes it's tougher pulling back and getting way from what we do, than it is to live the lives we are committed to...."

She nodded, straightened and brushed away the tear. But she did not leave my side.

"I am sorry, my dear. Sometimes I feel things too much."

"That's what these times are for, Eve—meditating, trying to make some sense out of it all."

"If that can bring the mind to a better place, yes," she said. "You are very good for me, my warrior."

"We're good for each other," I grinned at her. "I'm going inside to build a fire."

She arose with me. We walked back to the rental cabin, along a winding trail that climbed from the water, strolling hand-in-hand like first lovers.

It had been that pure.

"Most people can never reach out and touch what is here like you can," she said. "But you have these matters that have been troubling your mind?" Her golden Latin countenance beamed with all the sexuality and good humor of her race: "I see that my big norteamericano *is no longer plagued by thoughtful silence. Have your own troubles resolved themselves?"*

That was Eve, yeah.

Always caring.

"I'm going to accept a deal that's been offered," I told her. Then we went into the cabin and made love.

An evening to remember, yeah.

A woman Bolan could never forget.

He had decided that accepting Hal Brognola's offer was not a shifting of priorities, merely a broadening of the Executioner's scope.

Mack Bolan became John Phoenix and the Executioner's new world war against fanaticism was born.

Since that time, and the formation of the Stony Man Farm operation, the missions handed over by Hal Brognola had come hot and heavy. There had thus far been sixteen assignments for Colonel Phoenix and company, including the fledgling Phoenix Force.

But yeah, Mack Bolan still remembered that last time with Eve Aguilar, with clarity and yearning.

April Rose had then entered Bolan's life and Bolan never did have the opportunity to discuss April with Eve.

Evita dropped out of sight following the Smoky Mountain rendezvous, probably into the work for her government that had eventually taken her into Leonard Jericho's unholy operation.

At the time, Bolan had not been overly concerned. It was her job. Each of them had many times dropped out of sight from the world for months on end.

Mack Bolan reached the ridge of a dark dune that overlooked a downhill slope toward Aujila oasis and the base under the star-studded Libyan night.

Eve was there. It figured. He was sure. Big Eve, yeah.

Bolan had been calling her that since they first met because Evita Aguilar reminded him of the very first Eve. Eve had eaten of the apple of truth and become banished forever from the fairyland Garden of Eden of hoped-for "normalcy." During that transformation, Evita Aguilar had evolved into the only kind of woman that Mack Bolan could ever love. Like April, she understood that *gentle* did not mean *soft*; that *hard* did not mean *bad*.

And now . . . they had her.

Jericho and Santos the Butcher.

Inside the base that now stretched out before him.

Activity at the base was more distinct. But Bolan's view was blocked by towering oasis palm trees that thickly surrounded much of the installation.

He would need a better look.

19

Bolan was splayed out flat, elbows anchored in the hard desert earth, steadying his vision through the Starlight spotting scope.

A bitter night wind cut in from the north. Sand hissed along the desert floor, playing with the strands of his hair, stinging his face like thousands of pinpricks.

He was scouting the terrain with a slow panning motion. The Aujila oasis, and the Libyan army base that occupied most of its acreage, were clearly defined in the Starlight's greenish glow.

He advanced on a zigzag course. When he had followed the sloping descent of the terrain to a point three hundred yards north of the base perimeter, he flattened himself to the ground again and commenced a more detailed inspection of the installation and its environs.

From Bolan's position, the land leveled off for two hundred yards of rocky flats before the shadows of shrubs sprouted haphazardly for another thirty yards, when denser desert vegetation began thickening.

An advancing force of any size would have been detected. But one man, of Mack Bolan's capabilities, could attempt far more.

Generally, an oasis in this part of the Sahara would host quite a degree of activity catering to the nomadic Bedouin tribes who roam the land, or the occasional intrepid traveler who might stop to rest.

Aujila oasis was deserted of any human habitation except for the outpost. To the southwest of the installation stood the abandoned huddle of a *douar*, a native village of about seven *mechtas*, the mudwalled Arab houses, centered around a well beneath a cluster of shaggy, plump-topped date palms. The previous citizens had most likely been evacuated by government troops when the base was under construction.

Bolan could hear the dry rattle of the palm fronds in the breeze, and it was the only sound from that direction.

Inside the installation's outer perimeter fence, all shadows were dispelled by the merciless glare of powerful spotlights placed on tall steel posts.

Bolan read the north perimeter as their weakest point.

The base was a rectangle two hundred yards by one hundred and fifty yards. The main gate, at the southeast corner, was watched over by a gatehouse with, by Bolan's count, four military guards all armed with AK-47s. Bolan could see no other breaks in the barbed-wire-topped fence that surrounded the base.

A parade field in the center of the compound was squared off by the placement of three buildings (headquarters building to the north, motor-pool garages to the east and what must have been the CO's residence to the west) with the fourth side of the square being a broad tarmac crowded with what Bolan made as Soviet-manufactured implements of war, tarp-covered to avoid notice from passing aircraft.

From his angle on the ground, Bolan easily recognized the tell-tale outlines of twenty T-62 tanks armed with 115mm smoothbore cannons. He could make out the lines of another two dozen BMP armored personnel carriers, which he knew to be armed with 73mm antitank guns.

Too much damn equipment for a mere company of men, even a company of armored cavalry.

This confirms Lansdale's intel, thought Bolan. Colonel Shahkhia was fronting a Soviet-instigated coup against Khaddafi for sure. The remote base at Aujila was the rebels' arms depot, or one such depot, for the planned overthrow. All of the men soldiering the Aujila base would be rebels paid well for their loyalty by Shahkhia and the Russians.

Bolan saw a two-man patrol team by the cache of Soviet hardware, but no other activity in that area.

Most of the activity onbase was centered on the parade field that now doubled as a landing area for the two Hueys. One had carried Doyle here, away from the desert skirmish with Bolan and Hohlstrom.

The matching chopper could only belong to Leonard Jericho's party. They would all be in a rush here now, because of the actions in the desert that had upset the orderly progress of their terror.

The full company of base personnel appeared to be standing in formation, not far from the two choppers on the parade field. Every enlisted man, standing at parade rest, was armed with an AK-47.

Bolan could see Doyle's three mercs and pilot. No sign of Doyle himself.

But yeah, that was Doyle's chopper.

The cargo of Strain 7 was here.

Which meant Lenny Jericho—the real Lenny Jericho—was also here.

And Santos.

And Eve.

Bolan sensed vibrations of expectancy in the atmosphere of this Libyan base that were so strong as to be almost tangible. He could sense it through the Starlight scope at three hundred yards.

They were waiting down there.

Not for Bolan.

But, yeah... waiting.

Waiting for Colonel Shahkhia.

There could be some personnel in the barracks that backed the east perimeter who might spot a silent intruder. Another low, elongated structure running behind the barracks, the garage of the motor pool, could also have a crew on duty.

Bolan decided against penetrating the base from

the west. There stood the commander's residence, of Moorish stone architecture, where Leonard Jericho and Doyle would be awaiting Shahkhia's arrival. The command house would be well guarded.

He must not tip his presence here at any cost until after he located Eve Aguilar.

If she was here.

If she was alive.

He also ruled out an approach from the south, since such a strategy could get him seen by the guards at the main entrance gatehouse, who would be especially alert tonight.

This left as his only real option an approach on the stretch of fence behind the two-story HQ building. It would be near-vacant, with all the base brass in parade field formation, awaiting Colonel Shahkhia's arrival. This was a big moment for the rebels. The building would be empty except for a skeletal crew on duty in the CQ room.

The headquarters building would have detention cells.

He would find Eve in that building.

In a windowless "interrogation room."

Bolan's throat constricted at the thought.

He tucked the Starlight scope into his belted pouch and moved out.

The detailed recon had consumed less than thirty seconds.

He sprinted the stony slope of the knoll toward the outer reaches of the oasis. He soundlessly covered the flat stretch of rock and shrub and pale grass. He paused when he reached the base of one of the many outlying palm trees.

The chain link perimeter fence was another two hundred yards across dense shrubs and a turf of healthier grass.

From his present position, the penetration specialist's initial impression confirmed that there was no activity around the back of the administration building, fifteen yards inside the fence.

Bolan spotted a three-man roving patrol just outside the fence, walking east to west away from him. He waited until they had rounded to the western perimeter of the base and were out of sight. Then he left the cover of the palm and darted through the night toward the fence.

He met no interference.

He reached the foot of another palm with its trunk a short two yards from the installation's perimeter.

Bolan climbed the palm tree, rope-climbing style, working his way up to where the trunk curved, fifteen feet off the ground.

One of the tall steel lightposts, accommodating two of the powerful lamps that illuminated the area, towered up from a point fifteen feet inside the fence.

Bolan propelled himself in a free-fall away from the trunk of the palm tree, reaching out as he became airborne.

Two heartbeats, and his fists wrapped around the crossbar of the lamp post, breaking his fall as he

rode with the gravitational pull, swinging underneath
the crossbar like a trapeze artist, releasing it at exactly the right instant as he flew, feet first, into this new
hellground.

At the exact same beat of time, a roving three-man
patrol, dispatched since Bolan's recon, came strolling
around the corner of the headquarters building, less
than ten paces to Bolan's left. All three Libyan regu-
lars were toting AK assault rifles.

Bolan was still airborne.

The sighting was instantaneous on both sides.

20

The three Libyan soldiers had flaring moments to register some sort of reflex as the black-clad figure sailed in at them from out of the night sky.

It was all Mack Bolan gave them time for.

The Executioner twisted his body in flight at first glimpse of the guard patrol. He came in at the point man with a far-outreaching, stiff-legged kick to the guy's forehead that impacted skullbone into brain matter, ending that soldier's existence.

The two flank sentries fell away to the side, their eyes white and wide in the glare of the lamps as they fought time, slinging their AK-47s up and around on the invader who had already struck death and was now hitting ground with catlike grace.

Bolan executed a smooth roll that brought him up to face them in a low crouch, the silenced Beretta pulled and popping 9mm kisses of doom.

The sentry to Bolan's left caught a hot pill up his nose and out the back of his head. Bolan registered a death flop as the man pitched backward. Then his attention shifted, with the Beretta, to the second soldier. He could not afford any alarm raised at this time.

The Belle chugged again. Like the preceding sounds, the small handgun's husky sneeze was absorbed amid the steady hubbub of the army base around them.

The 9mm death round checked the rebel soldier's last move toward survival, a sidelong lunge as he tracked up his AK. The bullet cored in one ear and out the other, turning the survival dive into a final skid into Hell.

Bolan did not pause to verify the hits.

There was no response from the other side of the building, where the two helicopters and Colonel Shahkhia's rebel troops were situated.

The Executioner moved off soundlessly through the night.

He had to find Eve.

He had to find Leonard Jericho.

He had to hijack the cargo of Strain-7 from the center of that parade field in front of headquarters.

Bolan was certain that the container for the live virus was sitting out there, right now, in the well-guarded Huey chopper.

According to Jack Grimaldi, the virus was being transported in a 1 ½ x 1 ½-foot metal box, with handles and a warning gauge on the outside, strapped to a shock-absorbing device underneath.

That cargo of Strain-7 would always be Colonel Shahkhia's ace in the hole, no matter how his attempted coup turned out. Shahkhia could whisk the unholy stuff away from here, to someplace where only he would have access to it, and it would be his key to power.

Bolan's starting point was the tarmac, beyond the barracks and motor pool structures to the south, where he had spotted all the Soviet military hardware.

He hustled along the back wall of the motor pool garage until he came around to the massed tarp-covered weaponry.

This cache of hardware would serve Bolan perfectly as a diversion.

Bolan found the T-62 tanks and the BMP armored personnel carriers parked together in their own tight cluster. Not bad at all. It took him all of twenty-seven seconds to plant enough plastique explosive to blow the entire arms cache sky high. The detonators would be radio-triggered from a little black box, the size of a matchbox, which Bolan pulled from its belt location where Grimaldi had stashed it with the plastique and slipped into one of his blacksuit pockets as he moved out. His work here was done.

He had just quit the periphery of tarp-shrouded shadows when he came face to face with two more patrolling guards who entered the scene from the southeast corner of the motor-pool building.

Bolan terminated the rebel soldiers with waist-level shots that pitched both men into a tangle of death.

He zigzagged away from the encounter, retracing his way across the floodlit stretch behind the elongated motor-pool structure, heading back north in the direction of the headquarters building.

He glanced at his wristwatch as he trucked along. Two minutes and forty-two seconds had elapsed since breeching the security of this place.

Six men were already dead and Bolan knew they were only the first.

He swung around the north corner of the motor-pool garage, and several more yards brought him to the back entrance of the HQ building.

Bolan tried the door.

Locked of course.

He stepped back, cocked a foot and kicked the door in at lock height, the metal panel busting off its hinges, flying inward with Bolan the Executioner coming in right behind it.

A foyer. The CQ office was through an open adjoining door. A hallway reached off the length of the building.

Bolan entered the CQ office.

Two Libyan soldiers were manning the Charge of Quarters watch that is military SOP the world over. Both were visible from the doorway and responded to Bolan's sudden entrance.

The man seated behind a desk reached for a holstered pistol that rested on the desktop inches from his fingertips. He never touched it. He took a silenced 9mm death-dealer from the Beretta in the throat. The rebel was already a corpse when he slammed back into a wall map of Libya behind the desk, splattering the map.

Soldier number two had been sitting in a chair next to a coffeepot with his heels hooked on the window sill, gazing out on all the activity on the parade field. He was now drawing a snub-nosed handgun.

Bolan was near enough to chop down his Beretta hand with a sharp slash. Wristbone snapped loudly and the soldier howled in pain, dropping his gun.

The soldier took one look at his dead buddy and forgot his own troubles. He only had shocked eyes for the imposing figure in Executioner black who stood before him.

Bolan eyed the injured rebel down the length of an extended arm that ended with the snout of the Beretta.

"Where is she?"

The soldier's eyes were frantic. He spoke English, as did many Libyans.

"The man, Santos...he has her in the basement...do not kill me!"

"You brought yourself here," said Ice Voice.

The Beretta spat. The cannibal went down to join his dead friend.

Bolan swung away. A quick glance down the hallway that stretched before him showed a stairwell at the far end of the corridor.

He moved toward those stairs, swift and careful, passing other doors, some open, some closed.

He paused when he came to the armory. He stepped inside, reaching for more plastique. There was no one in sight. Most of the long room was row after row of empty racks. The soldiers awaiting Colonel Shahkhia's arrival were armed with the rifles that were kept here. But the rebels had left behind several Sagger AT-3 antitank guided missile launchers and Soviet 82mm mortars, as well as walls of stored ammunition.

Bolan sacrificed another twelve seconds from his numbers to plant one more clump of plastique. When the timer fuse was set, he continued on.

So far, so good.

But still much to do. . . .

The building was silent and lifeless around him, like a tomb. His footfalls echoed faintly.

He approached the stairwell. He eased open the metal door. A lighted stairway slanted downward for fifteen steps, then doglegged to the right.

Santos the Butcher was down there.

With Eve.

Bolan quietly closed the stairwell door behind him, then descended the stone steps, his back to the wall, the Beretta up. The stone wall felt cool, damp against his shoulders. Man and weapon were ready for whatever lay around that dogleg at the bottom.

He heard the murmur of voices speaking English.

He reached the bottom step and eased an eye around the corner for a look.

Three of Kennedy's American mercs stood guard in a boxlike, earthen-floored passageway to a closed door behind them.

These boys weren't outfitted with anything exotic. They carried .357s on their hips. Two toted Thompson submachine guns, the third held a pump shotgun. Back in the States, they would have been cheap Mafia street hoods. Maybe they were.

They certainly weren't expecting anything in Libya like Bolan. Two mercs were leaning back against the wall of the basement. The third man, with a tommy-gun, stood with his back to the wooden door they were guarding.

They were smoking cigarettes, conversing in words too low for Bolan to overhear.

Then he did hear something.

It was a sound more subtle than the murmur of conversation. It was a sound that burned his nerve ends raw.

A barely human sound.

A wailing moan of suffering that had no beginning or end: an eerie, modulating pitch that came as if from some weird musical instrument of the damned But it came, Bolan knew, from the depths of a living soul in torment.

A woman made those sounds.

Just behind that door.

Eve!

Bolan darted around the corner with the Beretta spitting lead.

The guy nearest to him was the first to spot the Executioner. He emitted a terrified yelp that drew the attention of the others. But he never got a chance to pull up his Thompson machine gun. Bolan's opening round caught him through his open mouth. There was no entry wound, but the 9mm parabellum needed more than skullbone to stop it. The wall behind the man's back-pedaling body was dirtied with a viscous red mess.

The guy with the pump shotgun fell away from the wall, trying to make a smaller target of himself as he tracked up the weapon in Bolan's direction.

Bolan's gunhand also tracked. The Beretta snapped off one chest hit and one head hit.

Bolan in penetration had gone undetected thus far—except by those who were dead—and if Bolan could dust them all without their fingers finding triggers. . . .

Which is when it happened.

And all secrecy was blown to hell by the hammering roar of the second tommygun.

Having nowhere to go but back, a defender had braced himself against the door he was guarding and gotten his chopper leveled at Bolan before two final bullets from the Beretta tagged him out of this reality.

But the dead man's finger had already tightened on the Thompson's trigger as death snatched him. The dying motion carried through. The dead merc sprayed off a wildly random, deafening burst. The whistling .45 slugs riddled the dirt floor of the passageway and ricocheted off brick walls, adding to the cacophony in those close confines. Then the guard's body collapsed and the brief burst ceased.

Far too late for Mack Bolan.

The echo of the reports still rang in his ears when the piercing sounds of an alert siren began sounding from upstairs and outside.

Sounds of confusion and movement carried with it.

It would be less than a minute before they found him down here. And his only way out was up that stairwell behind him.

The mission had gone *hard*. So be it.

And the moaning sounds continued from behind the door.

Bolan hurdled across the bodies on the floor. He slowed to holster his Beretta and snatch up one of the dropped Thompsons. Then he flung himself to the brick wall next to the door. The moaning sound was all he could hear. Something terrible was happening to a human being in there.

Bolan sent two hundred pounds of enraged kick into the wooden panel and followed through, storming in fast with the Thompson ready.

Into a living nightmare.

21

The room was a chamber of horrors, rank with the stink of torture. It was low-ceilinged, dominated by a surgical table with a bright light overhead throwing down a pitiless glare upon the thing that was strapped to the table; something...that had once been human.

Everything else was murky shadow.

Jericho had not waited to give her to Shahkhia. Not after things had gone wrong in the desert tonight. Jericho had needed to know immediately what Eve knew; he needed to know how endangered this operation was, and in how much danger he was putting himself by remaining here at the Aujila base, waiting for Colonel Shahkhia's cautious arrival. So he had turned her over to Santos for questioning.

The Butcher had worked fast.

Only the victim's long lustrous black hair, cascading over the end of the surgical table, denoted her identity. All else was a mutilated red slime, naked to the harsh overhead light.

Eve had been skinned alive from her head to toe.

Both eye sockets were hollowed bowls of gore.

But she lived!

She had no perception of Bolan's entry, or anything else.

The moaning sound came from a ghastly hole that had been her mouth.

Bolan took this in as he burst through the doorway. He dodged into the deepest shadows near the door.

Gunfire lanced out at him from the darkness beyond the table. A slug whistled harmlessly to his left.

The torture master had fired a too-hasty round and identified his position.

Bolan's Thompson submachine gun chattered off a full half clip, cutting to shreds whatever the room held...including an obese blob of human fat in a plastic apron stained with fresh bits of human crud.

Santos.

The Butcher was blasted into the circle of light as the heavy .45 slugs tore him apart, flopping his bloated body against the surgical table, then to the floor where it did not move, a rapidly spreading dark pool forming beneath him.

Santos would butcher no more.

But he had butchered this one....

Bolan felt so many emotions tearing at him as he turned toward the victim on the table that he thought he would explode.

The living dead spoke to him.

"*Q-quiero*...please..."

It was a voice from the grave.

Bolan felt hot tears in his eyes.

"Eve. . . my God, Eve. . . ."

"Please. . ." whispered a scratchy voice from that pitiful, butchered, ravaged person. "*Quiero. . . Dios. . .* let me die. . . ."

The moaning started again.

Bolan heard footfalls and equipment clanking as soldiers approached on the run from upstairs.

"Go with God," he bade her softly.

He ended her living hell, granting her last wish with a mercy round placed inches above the mouth-hole in the gory, skinned stump. And all he could think of was how beautiful she had looked that time on Lake Douglas. . . .

The moaning ceased.

A soul was released to Infinity.

And a bellow of blind rage screamed up from his warrior's soul, bursting forth, erupting into this foul torture room.

Bolan the human being lost all conscious track of time and action then. He would never recall exactly what happened during the next fifteen minutes.

A machine does not think in such a contemplative fashion.

And Mack Bolan had become a killing machine.

The thunder of approaching footfalls grew louder as they came into the HQ building overhead. A pause as the bodies in the CQ room were discovered. Seconds later, bootsteps came clattering down the stairwell.

The killing machine stepped out through the doorway, leaving the torture chamber behind, into the narrow passage.

Three soldiers charged around the dogleg at the bottom of the stairs.

The killing machine was waiting.

The Thompson stuttered in fury. Hammering bullets, on a sizzling firetrack of flame and smoke, blew away three rebels into piles of dead matter.

The killing machine moved on. Back up the stairs.

He reached for the small triggering device in his pocket.

As he emerged from the stairwell into the main hallway of the HQ building, he activated the detonator.

The night shuddered with sound and fury. A rapid series of explosions thudded from the direction of the armament and equipment stored on the tarmac across the parade field. A simultaneous blast from the armory blew out one wall into the hallway and shuddered the building to its foundation.

The HQ corridor, filled with billowing smoke and dust, now boasted four Libyan rebel troopers who had heard the gunfire from downstairs and were advancing two abreast toward the stairwell. The killing machine stepped out to meet them.

The guards had been ready for something, but the explosions from the armory room and outside still rumbled in their eardrums. The guards had glanced off in the direction of the noise. But they did not miss seeing the figure in combat black. They only missed the chance to do anything about it.

The killing machine hit the deck. The tommy gun blazed.

All four rebels died from a stitching figure-eight hail of steel-jacketed shredders that pulped the men into oblivion. It came from a being of cold eyes and hot aim. The enemy had no hope in hell.

The Executioner was up and moving out along the hallway in the same direction as he had entered, emerging moments later from the back door of the building, into the night.

The Executioner jogged a bee-line away from the admin building, toward the private residence that stood across five floodlit yards to the southwest.

A klaxton siren continued to blare.

Fires raged out of control from across the parade field where he had placed explosives amid the Soviet war machinery.

That equipment was now an inferno of golden tongues licking at the dark heavens.

The commotion of running men and shouting filled the night.

Most of the Libyan troops were breaking formation around the two Huey helicopters on the parade field and were rushing toward the fire.

A cluster of Leonard Jericho's mercs maintained guard around Doyle's chopper carrying the Strain-7, their Galils and Largo Star machine guns held ready as the mercs warily scanned the night around them.

The killing machine continued its course to the rear environs of the Moorish white stone structure.

He gained the back wall of the house and moved to a door. It was unlocked. He stepped inside. A short hallway. He heard voices and a shuffle of activity beyond a closed swing door in front of him. The killing machine pushed on through.

The big .44 AutoMag came unleathered as he covered the distance through an archway into what had been the dining room by original design.

It was now a command post in the process of hurriedly breaking camp.

The Executioner recognized Leonard Jericho. Two men were with Jericho. Doyle was toting a Largo Star. The third man had a slick, simonized American lawyer look about him. The lawyer and Jericho carried briefcases and all three were on their feet; they had been in the process of moving toward an entranceway at the front of the house.

All sensed the Executioner's presence and spun as one to confront him.

"I-I'm not armed!" screamed the lawyer.

"That's your problem," said the machine.

The AutoMag roared. The slickster died.

The giant handgun tracked next to Doyle. The number two merc's slate eyes registered panic as they realized he was about to die. He yanked the hi-power up from its holster. That was all. Doyle caught two rounds from Big Thunder. He died on his feet.

The body was still thumping to the floor when the last man, Leonard Jericho, raised his arms.

The renegade moneyman was in disarray. His eyes were rabid. The upraised hands trembled, as if trying to wave off his tab with eternity.

"No! Stop! I can buy you! Name your price!"

The killing machine in a single fluid movement holstered the AutoMag and swung the Thompson around into play by its shoulder strap.

"That's what the other Jericho said. The one I killed in the Bahamas."

This Lenny Jericho brightened. His breathing came faster.

"Carlyle. Yeah, I knew him. Hey, guy—*wait!* What makes you think *I'm* the real Jericho?"

"You'll do for now," grunted the Executioner.

The Thompson bucked.

And this particular Leonard Jericho was spun around by a flaming stream of millimeters that chewed his body into bits amid a curdling death cry. The steel-jacketed projectiles ate away at Jericho's death-jigging body, sections at a time, though the guy's final jig lasted less than ten seconds to pile his corpse into the corner.

This kill was for Eve.

Maybe machines could feel, sometimes.

Mack Bolan swung away from the execution. He quit the dining room, moving into the front entranceway, punching off every light switch that he passed, plunging the house of death into blackness.

When he reached the front door, he stationed himself against the inside wall.

He reached over and unlatched the door, drawing it inward several inches; enough to allow him a view of the panorama of parade ground and the raging fire beyond.

The two Bell Huey copters still sat side by side in the center of the parade field, thirty yards from him.

The Executioner centered his attention on the chopper carrying the cargo of Strain-7. Colonel Shahkhla still had not arrived. Jericho still had his security on tight.

Seven mercs stood guard near the aircraft that carried the living virus, their rifles held at port arms.

The killing machine quit the doorway of that house in a full frontal assault, Thompson yammering.

He must commandeer the helicopter.

He must lift the cargo of Strain-7 up and out, away to safety.

No matter what the odds.

The killing machine kept right on killing.

He blitzed five men between the house and the Huey. Two mercs were stitched in a tight pattern of blood before they even saw their executioner. Another came running and the Thompson sent him back-flopping across the paradise field with his head lifted away. Two mercs tried running for cover. They could not outrun the Thompson.

The Executioner reached the chopper as the pilot

tried to slam home the door and aim his .45 at Bolan at the same time. He accomplished neither. The Thompson erupted one more time and the pilot was ripped nearly in half by the hail of slugs. He dropped onto the ground beside the Huey.

Bolan leaped into the aircraft, slammed shut the side door on its runners and bolted to the controls.

He could see some Libyan troops across the parade field, by the burning equipment, who understood that a hijacking was taking place and were shouting out an alarm.

He gunned the engine and listened to the rising high-pitched scream of the revving transmission and the blades activating overhead. His fist tightened around the collective pitch-control lever to his left and he powered the big bird into a lift-off.

The commotion outside the Huey was lost below him.

He just might make it.

The pilot of the Soviet-furnished Libyan army helicopter, transporting Colonel Ahmad Shahkhia and two of his generals, controlled the aircraft into a hover position one half mile from the scene of battle raging below them to the north. The bodies of General Pornov and one of his aides were stretched out in the rear of the aircraft, with their throats slit from ear to ear.

Colonel Shahkhia recalled the icy premonition he had felt that afternoon when Jericho's people had informed him of the paramilitary hit on a Jericho base in the Bahamas.

He had felt concern that this action around the world might cause local repercussions in his dealings with these people. That was why he was being so cautious concerning his rendezvous with Jericho tonight, in spite of his whetted appetite for the female slave that Jericho had promised.

And of course there were Colonel Shahkhia's other plans for Leonard Jericho. . . .

Now a curt radio report from Aujila base had confirmed the earlier premonition. The communiqué sent word only that a sabotage team appeared to have them under attack.

Colonel Shahkhia had responded by ordering that all radio communications be cut and the full company of men down below be deployed to pinpoint this "team" of paramilitary penetrators.

Shahkhia was certain that the action had to be connected with whatever happened two days ago on Leonard Jericho's yacht in Exuma Cay.

The fires on the base below were spreading. Shahkhia watched with a constricting throat as the barracks and motor-pool structures caught fire.

Then the colonel saw an American Huey helicopter rising from the flames of Aujila oasis like some mechanical phoenix of war rising from the ashes of battle.

The virus.

The saboteurs were escaping with the virus!

Colonel Shahkhia pointed in his helicopter and bellowed a command that had his pilot goosing the aircraft into full-ahead thrust on a course of hot contact with that copter.

Ahmad Shahkhia understood the appalling chance he was taking. There was no way to ensure that the Huey chopper could be stopped without rupturing the container of Strain-7 aboard that machine. But the chance had to be taken. Shahkhia *needed* that cargo for what he planned. . . .

When their aircraft was some seventy yards to the Huey's starboard side, Colonel Shahkhia ordered his pilot to open fire with the Libyan copter's 40mm cannons.

The generals and pilot understood what was at stake. There was dead silence around the cockpit.

The pilot obeyed the command to attack.

The Libyan warplane sailed in on the Huey with both 40mm cannons firing steady.

The mighty hammering of the cannons in Colonel Shahkhia's ears sounded to him like the deafening approach of Armageddon.

The Executioner held the Huey at hover for a brief moment, once the copter had gained enough altitude to put him out of effective range of the rebel troops firing at him from the ground.

The raging tide of fire across the weapons stash and buildings below was like a sea of flame.

In the shifting, flickering patterns of light, the killing machine had one microsecond to see a Libyan chopper come zeroing in on him full-throttle from behind.

He yanked the controls, jarring his big Huey smartly into a sharp evasive maneuver at the same instant that the other aircraft's cannons opened fire.

The sound pounded at his ears. It enveloped him.

22

Jack Grimaldi, in the snappy Boeing 1041 V/STOL, entered the fray from out of the southeast. He confronted the Libyan chopper nearly head-on as they converged on the Huey piloted by Mack Bolan.

The Aujila oasis army base below them was nothing but a burning hellground of devastation and confusion.

One human being named Mack Bolan had been at work down there. Far larger than any machine.

The Huey jarred to its port side and fell sharply.

A stream of tracers lasered out from the Libyan aircraft's 40mm's into nothing but dark air.

The Libyan chopper banked around for another run and a look at the sudden unexpected arrival of the unmarked V/STOL.

Grimaldi sent a sizzling stream of bullets from his own 50-cal. machine guns after the Libyan army aircraft. He thought he saw a line of holes dotting across the fuselage of the chopper. But the Libyan aircraft was not stopped or even slowed.

Grimaldi raised Bolan on the tac net.

"Striker! Let's move tail outa here!"

"Not yet, Jack." Bolan's voice came strong and in command across the crackle of static. "That's a slice of Hell down there. We've got to level it."

"Evita? Is she all right?"

"She's dead, Jack. They made turkey meat out of her."

"Oh, sweet Christ."

"We level the dump," growled Bolan.

There was a metallic quality to the voice that Grimaldi had never heard before.

Grimaldi tasted bile trying to rise in his own throat. His knuckles were white around the V/STOL's controls.

Eve was dead.

The pilot had always loved that woman. Loved, yeah. The way a brother-in-law digs a sweet sister-in-law.

"Consider 'em leveled," Grimaldi radioed back.

He hardly recognized his own voice.

The Libyan chopper had looped back for more.

Grimaldi banked around, coming back to where Bolan's Huey held in a stationary hover.

The pilot of the Libyan chopper no doubt thought he had a good chance at taking them both with one blistering strafe run from north to south with the 40mm booming.

Grimaldi arced the V/STOL back into an evasive twist, the shrill whistling of the jet more piercing than before in his ears.

Bolan's voice crackled across the tac net.

"I've got him, Jack."

Grimaldi heard the Huey's turret-mounted machine guns crackle a tattoo that ultimately outlasted the hammering of the Libyans' fire. The Soviet-made chopper hurtled through airspace separating Bolan and Grimaldi.

Jack Grimaldi caught a sudden side view, as the Libyan helicopter thundered past his cockpit, of a man in a bemedaled military uniform, staring out from that chopper over his dead pilot's shoulder with a look of frenzied, panicky realization.

Colonel Ahmad Shahkhia was pounding his fists against the aircraft's Plexiglas window, screaming something as his chopper went down.

The explosion of the Libyan copter's fuel tank as it crashed below, out of sight, was only a dull *thud* sound to Grimaldi's ears.

Bolan piloted the Huey on a course toward the Aujila oasis installation. Grimaldi flew another tight pattern and came in too.

The Huey chopper opened fire on the base with its big 40mm cannons on full auto mode as Bolan swooped in.

Shahkhia's rebel troops down below were sent scattering and falling. Their ranks were decimated by the criss-cross of machine gun and air-to-surface missiles from above.

Grimaldi delivered hellfire and destruction with the V/STOL's full missile capability: three fast runs interwoven around the Huey's found targets.

The night shuddered with explosions.

The two attacking aircraft leveled every standing structure amid pandemonium born of erupting mortar and tossing human bodies and equipment.

It took Bolan and Grimaldi seven minutes to destroy the Aujila army installation.

When Bolan appeared to be satisfied, he banked the big Huey gunship off into an easterly flight.

Grimaldi did the same. They would both land soon and he would take aboard the big guy.

Eve Aguilar was dead.

Jack Grimaldi was still trying to absorb that awful fact.

As the fires of destruction receded away below and behind them, Grimaldi patched himself through to Bolan.

"Do you read me, Striker?"

There followed a longer pause than Grimaldi expected.

Then Bolan responded in that same iced metal voice.

"I read you, buddy. Thanks. Let's set these babies down. I want to get away from here."

"Roger. Mack, listen. . . I don't know what to say. About Eve, I mean. The bastards. . . ."

"I know how you feel, Jack. It's almost over."

"Almost?"

"I thought it would end at Aujila," said Bolan.

"That wasn't the last step. It's the next to last step."

"There's one more hit?"

"One more hit," acknowledged the grim guy piloting the Huey as the chopper and V/STOL continued their northeasterly flight. "There's a Tripoli address on the pilot's flight pad in this chopper. That's got to mean something. I'm going to find out what."

Cruising at three thousand feet through the cold Sahara night, Jack Grimaldi thought that if Death had a voice, it would sound exactly like the Executioner when Mack Bolan spoke those words.

Bolan did not continue the conversation.

Grimaldi signed off, leaving the big warrior alone with his thoughts.

All words were empty at a time like this, thought Grimaldi.

Only the pain inside was real.

Time magazine, in a cover story, had coined him The Most Wanted Fugitive in the World.

He stood at the half-open French windows of the penthouse terrace, overlooking the view of Tripoli by night, and chuckled at the thought of that magazine sobriquet.

Leonard Jericho had acquired such distinction without ever having killed a man.

He finished his drink, a very strong whiskey and soda, and moved from the French windows to the portable bar to fix himself another.

He decided that it might be a good idea to strap

on the Walther PPK .380 automatic that was now wrapped in its shoulder holster in the top desk drawer.

He would feel better, armed.

Leonard Jericho was a man of precautions. The nature of his business dealings placed him in a vulnerable position relative to various law enforcement agencies, to say nothing of his own business associates, past and present, many of whom thought they would, or could, gain much from his demise.

All due precautions had been taken, here in Tripoli as everywhere his dealings took him, including a guard out on the terrace and more armed men in the vestibule outside the front door of the penthouse.

And of course there were those two plastic surgery doubles he had used. There was Carlyle in the Bahamas. Gifford had taken his place at the Aujila rendezvous with Colonel Shahkhia. Jericho trusted no one, least of all treacherous desert rats like the buyer for that virus. Jericho would not be surprised if Shahkhia thought he had some foolproof plan for kidnapping "Leonard Jericho" at the oasis and holding him for billions in ransom. Jericho had chosen not to give Shahkhia the opportunity. He sent Gifford instead.

But there had been no word from the Aujila base!

Leonard Jericho sensed that something had gone wrong.

At this moment, he was awaiting word that his car had been brought around to the Tripoli safehouse from which The Most Wanted Fugitive in the World had been operating under the guise of an anonymous U.S. oil-company lackey.

He walked to the desk across the room and opened a drawer to reveal the leathered, small automatic... when he heard a peculiar sound from beyond the French windows to the terrace.

Jericho fisted his palm around the Walther's butt and started to yank the automatic from its holster as he looked up toward the windows.

When he did look up, the feel of that gun butt in his hand was the last physical sensation he experienced.

A figure in combat black hulked into the room from the terrace. The intruder's presence filled the penthouse like a jungle lord suddenly unleashed amid lesser beings. The man was heavy with armament. But at the moment, all he held in a one-handed grip was a long stainless steel AutoMag that was drawing a bead on the area between Leonard Jericho's eyes.

Jericho instinctively yanked the automatic from its leather, his senses short-circuiting with panic.

The .44 in the big man's fist belched fire in a strong grip.

And in his final microsecond of existence, Leonard Jericho had a crystalized curiosity. Would death be as powerful as the orgasm he had emptied into the Puerto Rican bitch last night on his private plane while Santos had done things to her with his knife?

Everything turned black with a hot splash that was no real pain at all.

They found Jericho's body minutes later, well after his executioner was gone. The skull was blown open. The top half of it was tilted at a crazy angle against the bar with brains staining the expensive carpet.

The real Leonard Jericho was dead.

EPILOGUE

From Mack Bolan's private journal:

A part of me died tonight.

The hurt is so bad that I can barely force myself to write these words. But I must write while the emotions are hot. These words are my grief.

The real Leonard Jericho is dead. His Libya connection has been destroyed. The Strain-7 virus is on its way back to the States, and so am I. And maybe, just maybe, the score has been settled for Eve Aguilar.

But the lady is still dead.

And gone forever.

And the only damn thing that keeps me going and caring at all right now is the knowledge that Big Eve didn't stop until they stopped her. She gave it all to the good fight. Everything.

Big Eve died for our sins.

For the evolutionary process.

Goodbye, lady.

I will carry you with me wherever the good fight takes me.

You meant plenty in life.
Your memory means something now too, by God.
Live on, Evita. Wherever you are.
It does matter.
It does.

MACK BOLAN

THE EXECUTIONER 49

appears again in
Doomsday Disciples
Coming in January, 1983
from Gold Eagle Books

One door closes and another opens.

When I put the Vietnam War behind me all those bloody encounters ago, it was the closing of a chapter in my life, but the story goes on. Instead of coming home, I found still another front in the war I had been fighting all along. Changing names and faces, sure, and the hellgrounds have a different set of longitudes and latitudes, but the mission has not changed at all. It feels as if I never left the jungle.

So the war does go on. It is a Terrorist War that I fight today, and it is the biggest war yet. Trace it back to Cain and Abel, to good and evil. I fight a holy war, make no mistake about it. At issue is the future of mankind. And there is no ground for compromise, no DMZ or sanctuaries for the enemy this time. Wherever he may burrow in, it is my task to root him out and exterminate him like the savage vermin that he is.

Yeah, the war goes on. The terrorists have written all the rules and taken all the bows so far, but now it's time to hurl back what they've been dishing out. Fire and steel.

Only the hot aim of my cleansing fire will reach the seed-germ of the plague and blast it to oblivion. Only I am free to purify the ground where poison drops and spreads.

The terrorists who contaminate us with their bloody guilt smeared across the headlines of a trembling world, condemn themselves by their own admission. They condemn themselves with their every word, every act, and I am not their judge.

I am their judgment.

> —from the journal of
> Mack Bolan, The Executioner

❋   ❋   ❋

Mack Bolan sprang into action as the flashlights spotted him.

He jerked open the Cadillac door and took the wheel.

Downrange, the limo's lights blazed on. Across the street, foot soldiers were advancing, firing as they came. The Caddy was already taking hits, leaden hail drumming on the doors and fenders.

A bullet struck the window post behind Bolan. Angry hornets filled the car's interior, buzzing in one side and out the other.

Bolan floored the accelerator. Tires smoked into a collision course with the limousine. He kicked on the high-beam lights, giving the enemy driver a taste of his own medicine.

The two cars hurtled toward each other. Bolan saw orange flames winking from the gun muzzles that bristled from the limo. One of Bolan's headlights exploded. His tank rolled on, a lumbering cyclops.

With heartbeats to spare before collision, Bolan cut the wheel and veered from the path of the oncoming limo.

Then the Executioner gunned the Caddy toward open road as the enemy driver stood on the brakes, fighting to turn the limo.

Bolan was halfway down the block when a garbage truck cut across his path. It had emerged from an alley, gears grinding, gunmen hanging off the back.

Bolan ducked as a fiery broadside erupted from the truck. The windshield shattered, raining safety glass onto Bolan's head and shoulders. Hot tumblers ripped the seat where his chest had been only seconds earlier.

He ripped the machine through a screaming turn, showing the enemy his tail. The gunners closed ranks behind him, peppering the Caddy's trunk. Bolan gave the tank its head and left the gunners in his dust.

He roared back along the block, running a gauntlet of fire for a second time. Hot lead hammered the car from all angles. Bolan raised the Ingram to dashboard level.

Ahead, the crew wagon was lurching through an awkward turn, coming around to face him, gunmen craning out the windows. Steady fire converged on the Caddy.

The limo moved to block Bolan's path. The warrior jammed his MAC-10 through the open windshield and lined up the target. Blazing steel-jackets found the limo's windshield, exploding in the driver's face. The driver's head snapped back, disintegrating in a scarlet spray.

Out of control, the limo veered away, scattering foot soldiers, plowing one over and churning him under the wheels.

Bolan chased the car with a parting burst, probing for a hot spot. He found it as the Ingram emptied out. The limo was transformed into a rolling chariot of fire.

Doors were flung open as a secondary blast rocked the dying vehicle. A flaming man staggered from the wreckage, screaming in a high unearthly voice as he collapsed on the pavement.

Nearly half the hostile guns were down and out now. The rest continued to track Bolan.

The Caddy's engine was knocking, the radiator steaming and the gas-gauge indicator was falling fast. The fuel tank was punctured. Soon the vehicle would die of thirst.

A gunner sprang into his path, blazing at him with an automatic carbine. Bolan framed the figure in his sights. The warrior's bumper took the guy low and hard, sweeping him off his feet and rolling him across the hood. It was a quick death.

Bolan reached the cross street and turned. A bullet blasted his right front tire.

The Executioner fought the skid, then was off and running clear, the Caddy clunking on the bare rim, leaving fuel and water in a steady stream. Behind him, the street was a parody of hell, complete with leaping flames and clouds of greasy smoke.

But Mack Bolan was clear, running with the wind at his back. Still in one piece, right.

For the moment....

Mack Bolan is a Winner!

Mack Bolan, captain of his own fate, protector of his own identity—Gold Eagle's hero blazes his way to success

"The Executioner books are action-packed!"
—Marketing Bestsellers

"The reading public knows what it wants, and it wants Mack Bolan. The Executioner books are real page-turners, packed with action. By any criteria, this is successful writing!"
—Dallas Times Herald

"Highly successful   a master of the genre"
—Mystery News

"Lines crackle on every page!"
—Toronto Star

"Action and variety!"
—Independence MO Examiner

"America's most successful adventure series. The best in the business."
—Navy News

His millions of fans applaud The Executioner, a warrior who affirms the sanctity of life

"You deserve some kind of reward for delivering such reading pleasure to millions of people throughout the world."

—*M.L.,* *Chicago, Illinois*

"Mack Bolan is a symbol to all of us who, if we were but half the man Mack is, would be out there waging our war against crime."

—*S.E.G., Baltimore, Maryland*

"I think my Executioner collection is the finest thing I own, or probably ever will own."

—*R.C., Gainsville, Florida*

Names available on request